De

This book is dedicated to Kit de Malplaquet
beloved son, grandson,
nephew and cousin your light shines
forever in our hearts

And to
my wonderful parents Maurice and Janette Placquet
who brought me into this world and provided the
Magik it took to bring this book
to life.

To Joss
Enjoy the Magik!
Love
Suzanne
xx

About the Book
Eddie Motion and the Tangible Magik

Eddie Motion is not like other boys, he knows exactly what people are thinking and feeling without them even saying a word. When a disturbing event occurs at school the impact propels him on an adventure to a strange land to uncover answers that will save his mother's life. Eddie was never just an ordinary boy. But until he is thrust into his mother's homeland of Andalustria, he has no idea just how magikal he is.

Eddie and his best friend Melody dive into an enchanted world where nothing is as it seems. Faeries bite, trees talk, ogres block the path and squiggins surprise them as unexpected friends appear and everyone, even you, seems to have magikal powers!

Suddenly, everything that made them different, even the bits they had thought weren't so cool, are celebrated. Unearthing the importance of accepting themselves in their truest form they discover how to create balance between their feelings and their thoughts.

As they re-discover their own unique gifts they begin to learn how to travel through the turbulent world wearing a new *'seatbelt of awareness'* to reclaim their true birth right and let their souls sing!

Eddie's 'Tangible Magik' helps friends to overcome the challenges set before them in the magikal land of Andalustria and it can help you too. Eddie wants to share his magik with you, so when you get to the end of his first adventure you too can dive into the 'Tangible Magik' toolkit, which can help you to understand how to create more of your very own special magik......

Acknowledgements

During the writing of this book I asked the help of several people who gave eagerly and generously of their time, knowledge and experience, I am truly grateful for that support and guidance.

This book would not have come into the light without the energy and wisdom of Tom Bird, I am forever grateful for his help re-opening the door to my creativity to awaken my own magical kingdom. My heartfelt thanks also goes to Rachael Jayne and Datta Groover, Monica Haynes, Karen Collyer, Susan MacIver, Libby and Sammy Ewing Jarvie who have all inspired and supported me to express my story out into the world in their own unique way.

Thank you for the support shared by my mastermind group and my many friends and supporters around the world, you have my sincere gratitude.

To my loving family who offered inspiration on this journey your support has been invaluable, thank you. My deep gratitude goes to my wonderful Godmother Jane whose loving heart and encouraging spirit is an ongoing support in my life and my adopted Godfather Chris Chown whose generous acceptance of life as it is always inspires me.

With extra special appreciation and very deep gratitude to my sister Charlotte Gaeta who has been with me every step of the way reviewing, editing, offering suggestions and acting as a prolific cheerleader above and beyond the call of duty.

I am also grateful to the shy introverted parts of myself that had the tenacity and courage to step through fear from behind the veil to bring this book to fruition.

My special thanks belongs to my very logical, practical husband Brent Masefield who not only helped me develop my characters, but revelled in their creation and the storytelling along the way, supporting and encouraging me at each turn, precious beyond words.

Eddie Motion

and the

Tangible Magik

Suzanne de Malplaquet

Contents

This paperback edition published in 2017 by
THINK SUCCESS LTD
Birkenhead Point
Auckland, New Zealand

2nd Print 2018

Book Website: www.tangiblemagik.com

Cover design by Monica Haynes; thethatchery.com

ISBN: 978-1-62747-183-1
eBook ISBN: 978-1-62747-185-5

Foreword

"Days of Devas, Knights of old,

Waiting patiently for your story to be told.

Life without you, is an Abyss,

Allowing you in, creates only Bliss.

Ground me now to work with Earth's Platter,

Enhancing my Life Purpose in all Practical Matter.

Uplift my Soul to Merge with the Heavens,

Give me Now the Gift of your Presence."

Suzanne de Malplaquet

Introduction

"To the castle through the forest, past the stream along knightly poplars, ready to feel all the way to your heart," said the guide.

Tall with long brown robes, long, grey, wavy hair, open-toed leather sandals and holding a wooden staff in his hand, he announced "Aaron is my name."

For so long had I waited to hear him speak his name . . .

Wanting, knowing he was there, but never daring to believe it was true, that this guide was here for *Me*. And yet they had always been here for me, in many forms and many lifetimes, as my father, brother, friend, to show me the way to my heart.

Earthen energy grounded me and made me feel safe. I know I am enough, I am loved and I am free when connected to my natural essence. Oh, to feel his presence all the time!

To know that I am safe in this often tumultuous world of constant change and transition is invaluable. He was the first to arrive to remind me of my true gifts that I had kept hidden for so long for fear of judgment, non-acceptance and persecution.

Chapter 1

Where Did Her Magik Go?

Edward saw how unhappy Mum had been since Rick her new ogre of a boss had started at her work; she always seemed uncertain and she said sorry *a lot*. He had overheard her crying late at night when she thought everyone was asleep but when Dad told her she could leave her job she shook her head and said no. Instead she took headache pills, rubbed the back of her neck constantly and said she couldn't leave her job as they needed the money.

Surely they didn't need the money so much that Mum had to give up and forget her magik and lose the joy of life?

Edward told her about Henrietta the spider, proudly showing her the beautiful woven tapestry of her web that shimmered and shook in the breeze. He held her hand and took her to the blackberry bush. But there never seemed to be any blackberries anymore and that only made Mum even sadder. He saw tears bubble up in her eyes as she glimpsed fleetingly into the past, remembering for a moment when she had lived in flow with life and the nature around them.

Edward tried talking to his father but he didn't really know what to say as he wasn't too sure if Dad understood about the magik that Mum and Eddie shared.

His father liked to fix things and was good at it; cars, machines, engines, and large metal objects were his father's thing. He had a special laser machine that made things line up and straighten so the machine could be fixed when it was broken and sick. Dad was clever, he could fix anything around the house, too. He made things no one else would ever think of, pulling them together out of what looked like nothing much at all.

Dad was considered a real hero; people called him to fix things all the time and paid him lots of money. He was always very busy. When he wasn't fixing things he was busy looking for and researching things he didn't know about, spending countless hours in his office and the garage.

Now Mum had lost her allure of enchantment his father spent less time with her. He knew he could fix cars and machines and was considered a real hero, but he didn't know how to fix Mum, and that made him sad. Had Dad understood about magik, he might have known how to help, but he didn't, nor did he know that Mum had lost hers. Only Edward knew this, and he was beginning to realise that only Eddie Motion could help here. But *how*? That was the question.

Almost a teenager, Eddie wasn't like most boys his age. While other boys did their best to appear confident and tough, swaggering rather than walking to school, Eddie loved to skip. As he made his way to school along the tall poplar-lined lane, Eddie wound his way in and out of those knightly trees in wavy squiggles. Around each tree he ran and skipped, running his hands over the roughened bark, twinkling his fingers through their feathery branches. He revelled in how the different textures felt on his sensitive palms, enlivened by his sense of connection with each of these majestic beings.

Skipping lightly and singing with the breeze as he joined in with the swaying trees, he felt at one with these natural beings he called friends.

Eddie was like a sponge to life and others feelings; his awareness of the seasons, textures, smells and the colours of nature was acute, allowing him to easily and effortlessly connect with animals and people no matter who they were.

There were few straight lines for this auburn-haired boy who felt the depths of despair of cold winters days one moment, then the joy and exhilaration of the sun twinkling on a dew drop in the next. He noticed the slightest shift of mood in the weather, as well as in other humans, feeling their sorrows and joys along with them, even when they didn't know that's what they were experiencing themselves.

Eddie was a happy boy, but the intensity of his sensory gifts and how he experienced life sometimes left him feeling overloaded. Experiencing and feeling life at ninety miles an hour meant he often needed to take a short nap as his heightened senses took a lot out of him. From a very young age he was wise enough to know he needed time out from others and their feelings and all he absorbed in life around him, so he wouldn't blow a fuse. He loved going into nature on his own, where there were no people to sense and he could replenish his energy.

Eddie was a surprisingly wise soul for his age and always took notice, listening to the messages his body sent him, so he could recognise what he was feeling in each moment. To Eddie things either felt right or they didn't. It was as simple as that.

Freedom of spirit was his natural gift, as he felt *everything* that crossed his path. He felt the fur from his little dog Missy, brushing through his hands as she ran alongside her human friend, mirroring his joy at every turn as he connected with nature and felt *all things*. Life flowed with and through him; he knew life was filled with wonder, magik and joy and he knew how lucky he was to wake up and be part of this magikal world each day.

To Eddie the sparkling dew drop on a blade of grass, the mist outlining the intricate matrix of Henrietta's web (his favourite spider, but don't tell the others), as it sparkled in the morning and evening sun lightened his spirit each day. He marvelled at the way his friend George the Ant gathered food from so many places, travelling thousands of ant miles to bring a wounded friend back home. He admired how George's family – millions of them – worked together easily without a cross word, just knowing and feeling their way with each other. Working as a team they could overcome mountains they never could have alone.

Then there was Mario the Magpie, who watched over his house, waiting for something shiny to show up so he could take it back to the love of his life, his wife Charlotte. She always waited patiently with her brooding youngsters, noisy in their eagerness to be fed. These were all part of his everyday life that made it so magikal.

Chapter 2
Oops, There's Melody

Skipping between the tall poplar trees on the path to school, Eddie was totally engrossed. Sensing everything around him with his hands, nose, eyes and his sensory heart, he felt keenly all there was to feel on this beautiful day.

As his thoughts turned to Mum and what he might do to help her recover her magik, he didn't see the girl riding her bike in a straight line along the pavement.

Bang, crash, wallop!

Legs went flying in the air, brakes squealed and the wheels of the now upside-down bike span around and around as Eddie Motion and Melody Mind collided into a crumpled heap on the ground.

"Ouch! That hurt," said Melody, quickly sitting up. She had fallen head first over the handlebars of her new bike. She had only just gotten the bike for her birthday, and loved its double bell, and special basket at the front.

Eddie thought she would probably call him 'Edward' now, as people tended to use his full name when he was in trouble, or they wanted him to be serious, which seemed to be often these days.

Melody Mind was a girl with jet-black, raven hair cut in straight lines. She liked straight lines in pretty much everything she did. For Melody things needed to make sense and follow a clear, focused path from A to B. She liked math, science and watching the stars at night. She was happiest when she had a mission, a problem to solve or overcome.

Melody wasn't into wavy lines or doing things "just because it felt right" as Eddie liked to do. She needed structure, routine and order to make sense of life and felt very uncomfortable without it. Melody was clever but she wasn't big-headed about it, she just saw life in a series of straight lines, which go backward and forward from where you are to where you want to go. It was so clear to her that she could never understand why other people didn't see this, too.

Melody had a level of intelligence that measured through the roof when she was tested at school. Although she didn't need to win at things, she did enjoy it when she did, and always needed to finish what she started. There were times Melody felt lonely as other people struggled to understand her, but most of the time she was okay with that, as she had Eddie as her friend.

Eddie sat up and looked at Melody, grinning from ear to ear as he looked at this beautiful creature with her bright blue eyes and shiny black hair. What a magnificent creature she was, she rode her bike just like she did everything, in very straight lines.

Eddie loved Melody, she was the best friend anyone could ever have, even though she didn't know it. Melody didn't notice how people felt, or the sparkling dewdrops on the grass or the twinkle in Mr. Owl's eyes when he winked at you just as you went off to bed.

But she did notice the stars and the moon and told Eddie she would go there one day, which he knew she would, as Melody always kept her word. Eddie felt

Melody had her own kind of magik, even if it was different from his.

Eddie and Melody had known each other since the first day of kindergarten and were soulmates from the moment they met. Even though they were so different and their experience of life seemed opposite on the surface, they had a common bond of deep appreciation for what each gave to the other, as it filled a gap that neither knew they had.

Sitting on the ground with a gashed knee and sore elbow, Eddie noticed Melody's books had fallen out of her basket and were spread right across the road. As he rushed to pick them up for her, Melody hooted and howled with laughter at the sight of the dishevelled boy in front of her. How Eddie made her laugh, something Melody rarely did unless she was with him.

It was easy with Eddie, he accepted without question that she liked straight lines, that she didn't always like to be with people and needed time on her own. He knew she didn't find talking to other people easy, and preferred reading her books and looking at the stars. He made her feel normal and safe, unlike some of the other kids at school who called her "special," but not in a good way.

Eddie thought she was special in a perfect way; he loved and accepted Melody and thought she was wonderful just as she was. In fact, he let her know she had her own special powers.

Eddie thought that Melody working out problems and being good at math and science was brilliant as she helped him understand these things in a simple, fun way, which none of the teachers had ever managed to do.

Melody knew Eddie was special too, in his own wonderful way, as he saw things other people didn't, just as she did. Even though what they saw and experienced was different from each other, their "specialness" bonded them with a deep connection that enabled each of them to know life wasn't just okay, it was really good.

They both knew that even if you only had one person, creature or being in the world who "got you" even if they didn't completely understand you; who accepted and believed in you as you were and saw your unique value where others couldn't, then that was more than enough to help you believe in yourself.

What a wonderful start in life they had been given, finding friendship in their opposite natures; helping to understand and accept differences and showing them how to love, cherish and believe in themselves, no matter what. The strong foundation they'd developed together set them apart from others. It set them both up well for life in this transient, sometimes unkind, and scary world.

Melody and Eddie were pretty unusual in that they knew they were special and were happy and proud to be so. Eddie saw the good in all people, things and animals; Melody observed and noticed how things could be fixed, seeing problems that Eddie rarely even noticed.

Eddie showed Melody that people weren't always scary, overwhelming or unkind and that when you felt scared, angry, lonely, or tired, that sometimes you didn't have to fix it or find a solution, as it wasn't wrong it was just how you felt. However hard it was to feel these things, Eddie taught her that if you just sat with the feeling, breathed into it and allowed it to flow through you it would soon pass.

Eddie taught her that when you sat or lay down on the ground and felt the earth beneath your body, or hugged a tree, or stroked an animal, you could feel calm pretty quickly.

He taught her to run her hands and feet under water and imagine the feelings she didn't like flowing away with the water. He told her no matter how upset you are, it feels good, because you could take charge and simply wash all the bad feelings away so you didn't have to feel awful anymore.

He called his insights and simple formulas "Tangible Magik."

The beauty of all of Eddie's formulas was that they were easy and simple to do and gave you very definite, practical action steps to take in any moment you needed them. When done consistently, they created astonishing transformation in your life on so many levels. Melody liked this about Eddie's notions and formulas and when she practiced them the results were indeed magikal, which pleasantly surprised her every time!

Eddie taught Melody many things for which she was grateful. She never questioned his wisdom about such matters, any more than he questioned how she understood math and could read complicated maps before she was five, and easily found her way home using the stars when they got lost in Mandelay woods once. He knew Melody would know how to fix the spoke on her bike that poked out dangerously after their collision.

When Eddie felt sad about his Mum losing her magik Melody would sit with him, quietly placing her hand on his knee. She let him talk and talk and cry and "should" all over the place as he jumped up and down, all the while quietly holding the space for her friend to express his feelings, even if she didn't totally understand them herself.

People mistook Melody's blank look, her focus on straight lines, her quiet reserve and passion for finding solutions as uncaring. Most struggled to relate to Melody, as she scared them, so they pushed her away. For many she was just too clever, too quiet, too uncomfortable, but not for Eddie.

Eddie Motion always owned his own feelings, he felt all his feelings and didn't make them about anyone else. He knew inherently that his feelings were his, and he was the one who could do something about them. He knew that people were uncomfortable with Melody only because they thought she was responsible for them feeling uncomfortable when they didn't know how to relate to her, which was not true.

Eddie knew that only when you take responsibility for your own feelings can you do something about them.

Eddie felt sad for people who didn't realise that no one can make you feel anything, that only you can think the thought that makes you feel a certain way about someone or something. He knew that when you knew that, really knew that, you could capture your own magical power and choose to feel how you want to feel regardless of the situation.

Eddie knew that you can't always control what happens to you, or how you feel in any moment, but you can always take charge of yourself and decide how you respond to a feeling, a person, or a situation.

Eddie loved Melody and Melody loved Eddie. Both knew they gave each other total permission to be their best selves. Together they learned to feel into life and think things through, so they could really enjoy each and every day, in their own special way.

As Eddie picked up Melody's books, he noticed a book he'd never seen before, *Find Your Way Through the Maze*. As he held it in his hands he could feel he was getting hotter and hotter, and tears sprang into the corner of his eyes. Was this a sign? Eddie was into signs, big-time.

Melody was able to solve puzzles and problems other people spent days on. She could see the road to get through the maze, mainly because she didn't let her emotions get in the way of seeing what needed to be done.

Maybe Melody could help him to get Mum's power back. If only she could, if only that was possible. Maybe this book could help?

He was just about to ask her when the school bus drove past and one of the teachers called out of the window, "Hurry up you two, quick smart, you'll be late for school."

They pulled themselves and their belongings together and walked as fast as they could with Eddie limping along and Melody quietly walking beside him.

"Melody, could you help me to help Mum find her magik?" he asked as they hurried to school.

"Of course, Eddie, we'll talk about it later," she said.

Chapter 3

Something Bad Happened at School

Later ended up being a lot later, as their day filled with activities and lessons focused on things that were supposed to be good for them.

They were half-way through a math lesson when a high-pitched bell began ringing loudly throughout the school. It went on and on, drowning out anything and everything else.

Then suddenly the siren went off, blasting their ear drums. They knew there was an emergency drill; they'd been told about it before but what was it they were supposed to do? The continuing noise from the bell and the siren were ear-piercing, rattling Eddie's brain and scattering his thoughts so he couldn't remember a thing. Fear raced through his body and froze him to the spot in shock.

The teacher shouted something, but no one could hear her above the alarms. Terrified children started running around, not able to hear the teachers' instructions and totally forgetting the drill they'd been shown previously.

Some cowered under their desks, others froze, one hid in a cupboard, and a few of them ran outside.

Melody saw Eddie freeze, his upright body looking like a rigid Popsicle. His eyes bright with fear, he looked like a rabbit in car headlights, and she knew she needed to help him.

Melody stayed calm, focusing on the breathing formula Eddie had taught her, trying to remember what she was supposed to do through the noisy din of the alarms. She trawled through her computer-like memory, searching for the right solution for this situation.

There it was, "Drop, Cover, Hold." *Great, now let's get Eddie*, she thought.

She called to Eddie, just two seats away, but he couldn't hear her. His body, along with his senses, froze in terror and overwhelm. Poor Eddie, he was so sensitive and caring of others, so accepting of their faults, which was a gift for other people but rendered him helpless when his senses went into overload as was happening now.

The combination of the loud noise from the alarms and the frightened children running around randomly En masse had triggered a complete sensory overload for Eddie.

To Melody, it was as if he had blown a fuse and burnt out his energy. She knew many people experienced this overwhelm feeling at some point in their lives, as the busy world can be overwhelming for everyone at times. But she found it strange that most people were often not even aware they were experiencing it, as they had become de-sensitised to their own feelings, as overwhelm had become so much part of their normal life experience.

She noticed that instead of finding ways to release their feelings people ate lots of chocolate or chips, or got lost in TV and surfing online, or went shopping and bought lots of new things. She thought this was probably their way of trying to overcome the feelings of sensory overload, but Melody thought it really only made things worse for them.

Eddie had told her all about overwhelm as it had affected him before, and he'd shown her how to deal with it. At first, she wasn't sure if she believed what he told her, so she looked it up in books and on Google, finding the information and facts were true.

So many people didn't realise they were filled with emotions they hadn't released or expressed. They didn't understand that the constant lights from their computers and phones stimulated their brains in a certain way that made it hard to relax. They didn't know any of this, or if they did, they weren't sure how to make it better.

But enough thinking, she thought, *she had to rescue Eddie, now!*

She climbed over the upturned chairs to reach Eddie, who still sat immobile, bolt upright like a statue. Luckily, she knew what to do.

"Edward, Edward," she touched his arm calling his full name loudly as if he were in trouble with a teacher or his Mum. She touched his face gently with her hands, then his heart, then his stomach. She looked him in the eyes and gently shook him, "Edward, breathe. Edward breathe," she said as she touched his chest; then placed Eddie's own hand on his chest, and his other hand on his stomach.

"Edward, breathe!" she instructed him.

Her touch helped Eddie reconnect with his body enough to make his eyelashes flutter and he took a big gulp of air. Disoriented, his eyes flashed into alertness, as air rushed back into his lungs.

"Edward, bend your knees and feel the ground under your feet, and breathe," Melody continued to instruct.

This was exactly what he'd taught her to do to become more "grounded and centred" in her body, as he called it and it had really worked for her. Now it would hopefully work for Eddie when he needed it. Could it really help him when he was so stressed and overwhelmed? Melody really hoped so.

She repeated her instructions once more and suddenly, like flipping a switch, he was back with her. He was still clearly distressed as the siren and bells still rang out so loudly they could hardly hear themselves think, but he was back with her now and not frozen in shock.

"Eddie, feel into your body. Take a breath down to your stomach, feel your hand on your stomach, feel the ground under your feet, and come into your body," Melody instructed, just as he had taught her. Seeing how quickly Eddie was recharging and coming back to her now, she started to feel surprisingly confident in her ability to help him.

"Drop down, get under the desk and hold onto its legs," she told him. Taking his hand, she followed the drill they'd been taught, "Drop, Cover, Hold."

Although he still looked pale and shaken, he took her lead, following her guidance. *How interesting*, Melody thought, as she noticed how quickly Eddie's grounding formula had helped calm him so he could do what he needed to do. She'd believed him when he'd shown her how to follow the formulas he'd developed, as they *always* made her feel better. But she'd never really understood how powerful they were until she saw how quickly it turned things around for Eddie, even in such frightening circumstances.

The insights and formulas Eddie had created could help people take charge of themselves so they could manage the different challenges that occurred every day more effectively in simple practical ways. The results could be really quite magical, she realised.

He'd say to Melody, "Let's press pause on life and create some *tangible magik,"* which she'd learnt by heart. As she crouched under the desk she felt relieved. Even though he was still white-faced and visibly shaken, she knew Eddie was now safely back in his body and feeling calm enough to deal with the situation.

She had time to think now. *What was going on?* There had been more than four drills in the last few months, which seemed a lot considering nothing actually seemed to be wrong.

"It's just a practice," they said, "in case of fire, earthquakes, or bad people coming into the school," but this only made everyone feel scared and didn't make them feel safe at all.

Testing the bells in case something happened was okay, but there must be a better way to do it. What was happening at the moment didn't prepare us to deal with things, it just made everyone even more scared and upset.

No one seemed to know about Eddie's simple yet life-improving formulas, which could easily help calm everyone in this or any other situation. If they did know, they could take charge easily so everyone felt safer and more relaxed quickly. Sure, it took practice to build the "Presence Muscle" as Eddie called it, but they could easily do it alongside the "Drop, Cover, Hold" formula, as it would work very well in that situation.

She needed to get Eddie to share his formulas with the teachers and students. Or maybe she could write them down for him, as Eddie was a *"being"* sort of person who liked to experience things, not really a writing-it-down sort of person.

Maybe she could help Eddie create a step-by-step plan for the students to follow Eddie's formulas. Then anyone who got scared in difficult or frightening situations would know exactly how to quickly recover when strange, unexpected, or bad things happened, or when their feelings were uncomfortable or overwhelming, or if they blew a fuse. What a great idea!

Reaching up from under the desk, Melody grabbed her workbook and began writing down a headline" "Press Pause Tangible Magik Formula.: This was a great use of her time, she thought, as there was nothing much else to do but wait until they were told they could come out from under their desks.

After what seemed like a very long time the bells and siren stopped ringing and clanging and a deathly silence came over the room. Many students were still hiding under their desks, unaware of what had happened. The teacher ran out of the room to find out what was going on, leaving everyone to wonder in the silence if it was safe to come out.

Yes, they really could do with Eddie's insights and his practical formulas to use at school, Melody thought as she finished writing it all down.

When the teacher returned she told them it had just been a drill and there was nothing to worry about, but as she still looked worried, this didn't help anyone feel any safer. She told them they could all go home, which was most unusual and gave them even more reason to worry.

Chapter 4

Discovering The Zingledibod Tree

Eddie had recovered considerably by now, but still wasn't feeling his usual self. He was pale and his body had stiffened, not at all like his usual carefree, relaxed demeanour.

Melody decided it would be a good idea to take Eddie into the woods, as she knew it would help him recover. The creatures, trees and plants would help him as he always looked after and loved them so well.

Leaving her damaged bike at school, they set off on foot to Mandalay Woods that stood at the edge of the field. It was dark and foreboding at times, but it was also welcoming and filled with a magik that only they seemed to know where to find. Melody was so grateful to Eddie for showing her the magik that was hidden in so many things, magik she'd never really noticed before.

The magik showed up in the vivacious red, yellow, and green dotted toadstools scattered through the woods, and the tiny semi-transparent earth worms sensuously doing their wiggly dance along the ground as they boogied with nature's vibration.

Magik was in the graceful gossamer butterflies that seemed to appear just when you needed a lift, in the medley of beautiful bird song from the birds that flitted in and out of the trees. Like a painter's palette, the birds appeared in various shades of brown, black, white and green with red and green tips, blue or red breasted, with multicoloured beaks.

The moss on the ground felt like velvet under their feet and cushioned their bodies when they laid on it, creating a scrummy bed filled with comfort, peace and joy.

Eddie instinctively knew about this magik. He saw it everywhere, he marvelled in all the creatures of the world and they loved him for it.

Crossing the field that stood tall with grass just waiting to be harvested, feeling the cool blades brushing against their legs, Eddie sensed his body recharging. It was as if he'd been plugged into an electric socket as he felt nature's energy current rushing into his body, filling him up.

As they approached the woods a huge shadow cast over them and across the field. Looking up they saw an enormous black bird that seemed to be heading in the same direction as them. It looked much bigger than any they had ever seen as it passed swiftly overhead. Eddie who marvelled at all nature's creatures was delighted, here was another bird he'd never seen before showing itself! *How exciting,* he thought.

The sun shone high above the woods, the glistening light rays through the trees creating a cosy place filled with promise. Running barefoot into the earthy woods in front of him, Eddie felt the moss filled to the brim with recent rainfall squish underfoot as it refreshed his feet and splashed up his legs. The water began washing away the distress from the blasting sirens, the children's panic, and the sensation of blowing a fuse in his body.

He knew exactly where to go, to the big tree in the middle of the woods. It seemed to hug you as you climbed up its branches that reached right up to the sky, higher than any other tree in the woods. This wonderful tree had a big broad trunk with a gap you could easily squeeze into, so you felt like you were inside a deep cave filled with unexpected promises of adventure.

Eddie loved this tree and often headed into the woods just to give the tree a big hug. Eddie knew this tree was an enchanted tree, but he never knew the tree's name. Maybe he should ask today.

Melody followed behind Eddie, knowing exactly where he was headed, happy to be with him, as she had grown to love the woods too, especially the big tree. What was it about this tree that seemed to be king of all the other trees? What made this particular tree feel so gentle and understanding, yet so strong, safe, and majestic?

Logically, how she felt about the tree didn't make any sense. But she realised more and more that sometimes you didn't need to know why something felt a certain way, you just needed to feel it. That was another lesson Eddie had taught her, one that had worked well for her many times recently.

By the time she got to the tree Eddie was already hugging it. His face pressed against the rough bark, he breathed in the beautiful woody smell that helped him reconnect with himself. He began to feel centred in his stomach and experienced the strength and support in his legs develop, as he allowed the tree's grounding earthy energy to enter his body.

Eddie knew how lucky he was to be able to understand nature's wisdom and feel all the wonderful things he experienced. Eddie knew not many people felt as he did and how much they really tussled and battled with their lives. He knew people really didn't need to struggle so much, if they could just let go and really notice what was all around them, particularly in nature, even for a moment they would feel so much better. If only they could allow the magik in to help them in their lives each day.

Melody joined Eddie as they both hugged the tree whose name they didn't know, savouring the moment and the uplifting sensations they experienced in every part of their bodies. Melody found she didn't need to think so much when she was hugging the tree, that she felt very calm and relaxed in her mind and actually in her body too. She felt as if she wanted to float and as if she was part of the earth too, all at the same time. Oh, she loved how connecting with nature made her feel.

They looked up and saw the huge black bird sitting on the very top of the tree. It seemed to be watching over them. Eddie wondered what sort of bird it was, as he had never seen one quite so large before.

"Thank you, dear tree, for helping me recover and for filling me up and restoring my battery. I love how you make me feel, thank you," he said, "please tell us your name?"

Eddie spoke to the tree out loud, not really expecting to receive an answer.

"I've been waiting for you to ask dear Edward, thank you for being our friend. We all love you here in the woods, you are part of us as you share our magik with all who will listen to help the humans of this world," the tree spoke, in a deep earthy voice.

"We can all help each other if we only ask and share, it's not difficult really, it just needs you to have an open heart, which you have, Eddie Motion," the tree explained.

Eddie jumped back from the tree with a start. He was totally surprised the tree had spoken and very excited that it had answered his request.

"I am known as 'The Zingledibod Tree.' I am the leader of this forest, overseeing and protecting all those in my domain," the tree said in his deeply melodic tone.

Melody stood back dumbstruck, as she'd heard the tree's response too, which she certainly hadn't expected, even though she'd secretly hoped the tree would answer. She knew Eddie talked to animals, plants, and creatures, but she didn't know they talked back. This was the first time she'd heard any of them speak.

Her logical, straight-lined brain told her this couldn't really be happening. As far as she was aware there were no facts or science for what was occurring.

What did it mean?

The tree continued talking to them. "Edward, you have come here to recharge after blowing out your energy with the shock of what occurred in your world today. For you understand the vitality our natural kingdom offers. The wisdom and blessings it brings to all who share with and notice us helps you find your centre. For this we thank you, as in connecting with us, you recharge us, too. It's what we call a team effort. But I think you have another question you really want answered, do you not?" the tree asked.

Eddie was so inspired by the beautiful tree talking to him that it occurred to him he might be imagining it, as he had a habit of doing, at least that's what his mother said. But seeing the look of surprise and amazement on Melody's face, Eddie realised she could hear the tree talking too.

"What question do I have Mr. Zingledibod? I'm not sure. I do have a lot of questions for you, but I can't think of one in particular that stands out right now," Eddie told the tree.

The Zingledibod tree carried on, "I believe you want to know how to help your mother get her magik back, is that not correct?"

Melody looked at Eddie as his mouth dropped wide open, surprise and wonder passing over his face. Eddie was completely speechless. How did this tree in the middle of Mandelay Woods know what he'd been worrying about for so long; how did it know?

"The natural kingdom knows what you think and feel, as we're here to support you whenever you ask. It may not be in the way of the humans that we help you, but we hold the energy for you to work out what you need for yourselves."

"We're always here for you to connect with us through touching, hugging, experiencing our smell and seeing our beauty, as it all unites you with your heart. Your heart is where all your answers lie, it is the same for everyone. But unfortunately many people have forgotten how to go there. That is why we're still here to help you so you can connect to your heart and your true nature, so you can all be happier in your lives."

"We feel your energy and your vibration and can help you reconnect to your own natural rhythm which is your birth right, that you humans forgot long ago. You, dear Eddie, are a very special human, as you have never lost or forgotten your connection to your heart. That is why you are able to talk to us, to hear us, and feel us, so we can help each other as a team. You can help other humans remember their birth right too, when you're ready," the Zingledibod tree explained.

Wow! This was amazing, Melody thought. She felt in every bone in her body that the words the tree spoke were true. But her clever, very logical brain was just amazed by what was happening, as she had no book or fact to help her make sense of this right now.

Eddie felt really grateful to the Zingledibod tree. He believed what the tree said, even if he wasn't too sure how he could help other humans right now. None of them seemed ready to listen, nor want to connect with the natural kingdom in the way Eddie did – except Melody.

He thought Melody hadn't understood about all this when they first met, as she was only focused on straight lines and facts. But Melody had decided early on that she would listen to what Eddie had to say and try it out, because it was all very interesting and she knew that the only way you really knew if something was true or not was to try it out for yourself.

So now, after trying it out for several years, she understood how precious this information was for humans and how beneficial it could be for them if they understood the type of magik that Eddie was born to know and share.

Seeing was believing in Melody's world, so she totally endorsed Eddie's formulas, as they'd made such a huge difference for her on many occasions. After all, she'd quickly been able to support Eddie when sensory overload and jangled nerves overtook him earlier at school. Melody knew Eddie's tangible magik worked. *Maybe it could help Eddie's mother? Maybe it could help other people, too?*

"That would be wonderful," Eddie said with great relief, "can you really tell me how to help my mother?"

"I can't tell you how to do it, but I can show you the way to start on a journey of your own, so you can uncover what will help your mother. How would you like that?"

"Yes, I would, very much, thank you! Can Melody come, too?" Eddie asked.

"Of course! Weren't you going to ask her to help you, anyway?" the tree enquired. "As Melody is especially good at finding answers to problems and finding her way through the puzzles in life, she will be a great help to you. And I think Melody might learn a few things for herself along the way too," the tree encouraged.

Melody blushed. Having the tree praise her and recognise how helpful her gifts were to other people, especially Eddie, was lovely and made her feel quite valuable, instead of just interesting.

Melody knew in that instant, no matter what else happened in her life, she would always be grateful to the Zingledibod tree for truly understanding who she was. In that moment she knew she was perfect, just as she was, which is something she had never truly felt before.

What a prize Eddie had given her, opening a doorway into another world, so she could understand how to connect with the natural kingdom and with the creatures that seemed to know the true essence of each human and their gifts. These creatures seemed to know how to help them bring these gifts out into the world to help to make it a better place. But only if they were ready to listen!

"Yes, I'd love to help Eddie, what do we have to do?" Melody asked, excited.

"Dear Melody, take Edward's hand and step inside between the gap," the Zingledibod tree directed them.

"Chandor the Raven, the big black bird watching over you high above, will help you travel through the veil between worlds so you can uncover the answers you need."

"Chandor is the great protector; his gift of insight knows the truth in all situations as he traverses through time and space. He lives with the seer of all worlds who you will meet soon enough. He will oversee your journey now," the tree said in a reassuring tone.

They looked at each other, smiling nervously, comforted by the thought of Chandor watching over and protecting them. Holding hands, they squeezed through the gap in the Zingledibod tree's massive trunk.

They totally trusted what the old, majestic tree told them, knowing in their hearts that right now was the perfect time to begin this adventure.

"Hold onto each other tightly, as it will feel fast; like light speed. Take a really deep breath and close your eyes," the Zingledibod tree instructed.

The friends did as they were told without question; they just completely let go and trusted as they set off to who knew where.

Chapter 5

Guardians of a Strange Land

They felt themselves zoom into the air, their stomachs dropping to their feet as they moved upward, faster and faster. It felt as if they were flying through time and space, which made them feel a bit giddy until they got used to it.

Stars and lights flashed past them, then sun beams shone and glistened brightly as different countries seemed to whiz by as they flew ever upward inside the trunk of the Zingledibod tree.

They held onto each other tightly, both with big grins across their faces. Somehow they knew they were starting on the adventure of a lifetime and it was going to be a lot of fun!

It seemed to take ages but finally they felt everything slow down, then suddenly they arrived with a bump! Their feet landed solidly on the ground inside the tree.

Who knows where they were now? It all felt very strange, yet exciting.

It was as if nothing had moved and the inside of the tree was exactly the same as before. They felt as if they had been in a supersonic lift in a department store, going up to another floor, going so much faster than was usual, yet taking a lot longer.

"You have crossed through the veil between worlds, you can get out now," said the Zingledibod tree to the cautious friends.

"What should we do now, where should we go?" asked Melody, her straight-lined brain kicking in to take charge to help them on the next stage of this journey.

Eddie was quite happy to see what turned up and go with the flow, but Melody wanted to know what to do so she could create a plan to make the best of the situation. She could only go so long without a plan or some sort of facts to work with, before she felt a bit agitated.

"Dear Melody, don't worry. You don't need to be frightened, it will all become obvious. But I know you like to have a plan and some facts, so here's some information to get you started," the tree told them.

"Once you step outside, you will be in the land of Andalustria, where wonder and enchantment will surround you," the tree said.

"Don't worry if it's not what you're used to, they have their own plans and facts here. It's just a bit different from your home. All that you need will be provided for you, when you look and listen.

"You'll easily uncover the best way to go about things with your wonderful straight-lined brain Melody, and you're going to learn a lot that will be helpful with your research. You will be a great help too, Edward, with your natural instinct, insights, and way of reading situations," the tree encouraged them.

The Zingledibod tree seemed to know Melody and Eddie so well. He knew what Melody needed to feel reassured and he knew about her dreams and hopes, which encouraged her so she stopped feeling fearful of what was to come.

The tree had promised there would be facts, which meant she could create a plan to help them, but there would be enchantment, too. Melody believed in magik, she believed in the mystery of the universe and the stars, and she understood about the miracle of having someone like Eddie as her friend. She also understood about facts and figures and how things all came together when you had a plan, which was thrilling to her.

She believed in a different type of magik from Eddie, which to her was just as important. Melody thought that if she and Eddie combined and blended their gifts, as the Zingledibod tree was asking them to do, they could make the most of this adventure. It would be incredible to see what they could create together. With her clear, focused, logical brain and Eddie's highly tuned emotional instincts, imagine how powerful that could be, she thought.

"Now that you have arrived in Andalustria you can follow the path until a guide appears to show you the way. You will learn new things at each crossroad, river, mountain and stream, as there will be many helpers to teach you what you need to know," the great tree said.

"You'll also come across naughty, enchanting, and dark elementals that will try to have some fun with you. Some of these are very dangerous and need to be avoided at all costs," the tree warned.

"At times things will appear to be one thing but will turn out to be quite different from how they first appear.

So you need to be on your toes and keep your eyes and ears open and your wits about you. Let your unique gifts and your senses guide you so you're able to be fully aware along the way."

"If you become frightened or don't know what to do, use Eddie's tangible magik along with your clear, focused thinking, Melody. When you work together with your wonderful heart energy Eddie, alongside your wonderful brain Melody, true alchemy will occur," the tree spoke, mirroring exactly what had been on Melody's mind.

"You will be just fine, and you'll uncover the answers you seek, even if they are not as you expect," the tree said, bolstering their courage before they set off.

The friends felt very grateful to the Zingledibod tree for his guidance and reassurance as he outlined what might happen. The wise tree knew that every child and adult needs to be given an idea of what might be ahead in order to feel safe. Then they could work out what they needed to do to prepare themselves so they could deal with whatever happened.

All children know this deep down, but sometimes grownups forgot this and they tried to hide things from children because they believe they might not be able to cope with the truth. Sometimes grownups simply didn't know how to explain what was happening in a positive way that was helpful to a child.

But in many situations not being told about things and what was going on was worse than knowing. Just like the animal kingdom, children and adults sense when something's not quite right, which only fills them with more fear if no one talks openly about it, in a way that makes sense and can help prepare them.

The Zingledibod tree was indeed very wise!

When they stepped outside the Zingledibod tree they were met with a vision of bright colours. This land was filled with huge flowers and plants of every hue of the rainbow. Flowers of red, orange, blue, indigo, and violet and bushes and trees of every shade of green, gold, and yellow spread across the land in front of them. It was so luscious and vibrant and made them feel happy just to look at them.

They noticed that the huge flowers actually had eyes! The flower heads were winking at them and giggling as they swayed from side to side atop their tall purple stems.

The path underfoot was made up of thousands of tiny shiny pebbles that glittered and sparkled as the sun shone upon them. The pebbles tickled their feet as they walked, making them want to laugh with each step. As far as they could see the path ahead looked like a gold and silver carpet, like nothing they had ever imagined or seen before.

They felt a big *whoosh* of air breeze past as they heard the flap of Chandor's vast wings overhead. It was reassuring to know this stately bird was there to look after them as they started their expedition into this new and unknown land of Andalustria.

Ahead they could see the gold and silver glittering path leading into a dense forest that seemed to call them.

Eddie and Melody looked at each other with grins on their faces, full of excitement. This land with its exotic shades and fragrances, vibrantly uplifting plants, and mysterious pathways just calling them onward felt totally enchanting and they knew this was going to be an adventure they would never forget.

They said farewell to the Zingledibod tree and started along the path. Both felt as light as air, as if they were floating along the glittering path toward the woods, not worrying too much about the next steps or what would occur.

It felt freeing being in the strange and beautiful land of Andalustria after the Zingledibod tree assured them it would all be okay. Even if there were mischievous or dangerous creatures that might cause trouble along the way, it felt exciting to set off.

Following the path, they heard the tinkling of water nearby and noticed a stream running alongside them, caressing small rocks as it meandered toward the forest ahead. The stream babbled and giggled much like the flowers, but with a distinctive tinkling sound that vibrated through their bodies and into their stomachs, making them feel free and filled with fun.

As they got closer to the forest they could see curling tendrils of smoke swirling high into the air somewhere off in the distance. They wondered if it was a campfire or someone's home fire. What was awaiting them ahead in this deep wood?

Melody thought about how exciting it will be to meet the inhabitants and creatures of this land, and decided to do a study on what she uncovered in Andalustria for her research.

As they neared the entrance to the forest the tall trees started crowding closer together as if they were jostling with each other and they heard a rustle in the bushes nearby, then it stopped. They carried on, but stopped when they heard it again. This time they actually saw the bushes shaking vigorously; they heard the rustling noise get louder as they came closer.

What was it? An animal of some sort? A person?

Then everything became still again, so they kept walking toward the forest.

Just as they were about to take their first step into the forest, a huge, wizened creature jumped out and barred their way.

What was it? It looked like the pictures of gargoyles they'd seen in history books. Or maybe it was a strange-looking reptile they'd seen in fairy books, but a whole lot uglier.

The creature must have been seven foot tall. Its skin was leathery and a brown-lime green colour, just like a lizard's. It had long, skinny arms and legs with long fingers and toes that had really long, sharp nails.

The creature jutted its head forward, lifting its bright yellow eyes as it spoke in a strange language they'd never heard before. Its voice sounded guttural and nasal and its long forked tongue jutted out in-between words.

Eddie and Melody couldn't understand the creature so just stood there, which only seemed to make the creature more animated as it began to talk faster with more head-jutting movements.

Eddie raised his shoulders and arms in the air, gesturing to show he didn't understand what the creature was saying. As he did this, the creature mimicked Eddie and did the same physical movements, whilst tilting his head to the side.

Eddie knew that when the creature tilted his head slightly to the side he was interested in them, and probably wasn't dangerous. The fact that the creature had mimicked Eddie's body movements showed he was inquisitive, rather than a threat. At least that was what the body language suggested to Eddie, who was unusually good at reading it.

Had Eddie not known how to read the signals of the creature's body, it would have been easy to fear it. It was pretty ugly and sounded quite unusual with the strange language it spoke, making it appear hostile.

Melody was impressed as Eddie conveyed this information to her. She realised Eddie used facts to help him too, as well as his own natural instincts, which helped her realise how similar they were at times. In that moment, she loved her friend even more.

Eddie thought he'd try something, as the creature was copying what Eddie was doing. They needed to do something, as the creature was blocking their way into the forest, where they knew they needed to go.

Eddie sat down on a rock nearby, folded his arms and waited. Melody watched in amazement as the creature also sat down on a nearby rock and folded its arms, too.

Wow, things are taking a strange turn, Melody thought. This was really fascinating.

Eddie said his own name and touched his hand to his chest to gesture that this was his name, then he waited.

Almost immediately the creature touched his long, skinny, leathery finger to his chest. In his guttural tone said, "I am Ling, keeper of the forest. Where have you come from and how can I help you?"

It would have been strange enough if the creature had said this in its own language, but it said all this in a language both Melody and Eddie could understand, although it didn't seem to be English.

"How is it we can understand you, as this is not our language?" Eddie asked, excited that somehow he understood this new language, a language that he'd never known even existed before.

Ling answered, "Because you understood my body language, your energy has blended with mine, which means you can recognise the words and messages I speak. What you did confirmed to me that you wanted to understand and to know me, and that you are not a threat," Ling explained.

"You have made it possible to open the door between our two worlds with your kind and open behaviour and your willingness to accept me without judging me. So now we can understand each other on many levels, one of which includes our spoken language."

Wouldn't it be great if this was something that could happen between humans in our world! thought Eddie.

Just as Eddie was thinking this, Ling said, "It can!"

Eddie jumped so high Melody took a step back, wondering what the matter was.

Looking at Melody he stammered, "Ling just read my thoughts!"

"This is an amazing place! How did you do that, Ling?" Eddie asked the strange creature.

"Once you opened the door to communicate openly with me you let me in, as you showed me you wanted to be my friend, or at least understand me, not be my enemy. Then I could read all the languages you have. That means I can understand and read your thoughts, feelings, words, your body, and your spirit language. And you will be able to read mine too, once you know how," he explained to Eddie.

"Whoooah, that's incredible!" Eddie danced around, hopping from one foot to the other excitedly as if someone had put hairy hot potatoes down his trousers.

"How cool would that be!" he exclaimed, completely excited and inspired by the possibility of being able to read and understand all creatures, no matter where they came from.

Meanwhile Melody stood there watching what was going on as she worked something out in her head. Eventually she spoke up.

"You mean if we show others we want to understand them and their ways then an invisible door opens, allowing us to read their signals so we can create a connection and develop friendships around the world?"

"Yes," said Ling, "it's only fear and judgment that stops us all from understanding each other. Even if we look different, sound different, smell different, or behave differently because we come from another place, we can all learn to understand, accept, and care for each other, no matter who we are," he said passionately.

"Whether we are a prince or pauper, king or queen, human or creature, plant or animal, we can all get on together if we choose. It's actually not that difficult when you know how, and when you choose to be open to the possibility."

Although from a straight-line point of view this seemed unlikely to Melody, somehow she knew deep in her heart that the possibility of Ling's statement was true.

"Thank you, Ling," she said, "this is wonderful, to believe this could be possible for all of us!

"Thank you for opening the door for us to understand, even if we need to grow and practice developing this 'understanding, accepting muscle' so doors can be opened for us, it feels really good to know this is possible," Melody continued, moved by Ling's words.

"Thank you," said Ling, "as it was actually you and Eddie who opened the door for this to be possible because you came here to discover how to help Eddie's mother out of the goodness in your hearts."

"You came with an open mind, even though you were uncertain. You brought your own unique mind and heart energy here to Andalustria and are open to this new adventure and meeting new folks along the way."

"Interest, acceptance, and understanding are both your armour and your gifts, never forget this as you go on your way. They will serve you well," Ling said, acknowledging the children.

"Thank you for accepting me as I am," Ling said. "You will see me in many forms on this adventure and in this lifetime. I truly hope you will always remember this powerful lesson, as it will serve you well, dear friends. You may go on your way through the forest, we will meet again soon."

Ling moved aside, allowing them to continue into the forest.

Chapter 6

Vampire Faeries - Friend or Foe?

They left their new friend Ling with a spring in their step, feeling happier and lighter after learning about the importance of being interested, accepting, and understanding of others. Now they had a greater understanding about how best to communicate with the creatures of this land.

Eddie began to run and skip, taking Melody's hand as she joined him skipping along the path. Melody had always thought skipping wasn't for her as it meant going from side to side, moving away from the straight lines she loved so much. It had felt uncomfortable in the past, but after meeting Ling and experiencing what it felt like to freely accept and be accepted, she thought she'd give skipping a go. Perhaps she had been judging skipping as bad without really trying it. Wasn't that a big part of Ling's lesson, to try new things with openness and acceptance, realising that it is neither good nor bad, it just is.

She realised it was only what you chose to think about something that made it one way or the other. You can change the thought you have about it any time you choose, and for Melody that lesson was really quite exciting to learn!

Skipping along in a higgledy-piggledy fashion, she had moments where she felt like she was flying. It was quite unnerving, as it felt new and uncomfortable, but holding Eddie's hand and letting her judgment go she

42

started to understand. Skipping was quite good fun; it actually felt really good when she just let herself let go and enjoy it.

What else had her straight thinking held her back from trying? She was just beginning to think about the many things she might have explored, had she allowed herself, when they noticed Chandor the Raven circling high above them. He was a fair way off in the distance, which made them feel safe, as if they were being taken care of as they walked toward who knew what.

Shortly the glittering pebble path started to taper off and was replaced by a mossy track that felt soft underfoot, even with shoes on. Eddie, being Eddie, wanted to feel the moss under his feet. It was always such a wonderful experience when he re-connected himself body and soul with the textures, sights, and smells of nature. It always filled him with joy, a renewed sense of being alive and a deep calm, knowing that he really could do anything he put his mind to.

He felt the sponge-like sensation of the velveteen moss on the soles of his feet as they sank into the springy softness. A warm sensation moved up his legs and into his stomach as he experienced a deep connection to the earth whilst this wonderful green carpet caressed his feet.

Melody decided she wasn't quite ready for barefoot moss-walking; giving in to skipping was probably enough of a leap for her for one day. She was feeling a little uncomfortable, as nothing that was happening in this world fitted into her world of facts at all!

That didn't stop her from feeling happy though, watching Eddie's enjoyment as he bonded with nature. She knew it reconnected him to the natural part of himself in such simple, uplifting ways. She saw how it gave him heaps of new energy and a heightened sense of happiness as he fully embraced every new opportunity, as he saw the magik in everything, whatever it was, even strange creatures like Ling!

Others might have been afraid and thought Ling was a threat or an enemy. They may have run away from Ling or even attacked him. But not Eddie. He saw Ling for who he truly was, a creature who just wanted to be understood and accepted for who he was, just as they did. Melody thought that was all anybody really wanted.

Melody was recognising more than ever before that Eddie's childlike acceptance of others and whatever occurred in life, his willingness to try new things and go with the flow, looking for the good in each experience, showed a great wisdom that surmounted his size and age. *Many fully grown adults could learn a lot from Eddie Motion,* she thought!

Rounding a bend on the path, Eddie's focus was drawn to a cluster of what appeared to be fireflies wafting gently through the air just ahead of him. As the forest trees closed in around them, it became darker as the tall, majestic, green and brown wooden knights blocked out the last speckles of sunlight from the day. Their branches and roots entwined and danced gently together, huddling closer and closer the farther they moved into the forest.

Eddie was grateful that the quivering wings of the stunning fireflies appeared to light the way as they danced and floated through the air ahead of him.

As their eyes adjusted to the diminishing daylight and their senses became attuned to the darkening, damp, denseness of the forest, they noticed a flickering bright light off in the distance. It looked like a camp fire.

Melody wondered what was ahead. If that was where the swirling smoke was coming from, it might make a good place to head toward. They were chilly now, as the dampness from the earth seemed to seep into their bones. How had they not noticed it getting colder as the warmth of the sunlight disappeared?

Eddie carried on deeper into the forest, completely mesmerized as he followed the beautiful creatures that resembled fireflies.

He was totally captivated by them. Approaching closer to get a better look, he realised they were tiny faery-like people. They seemed to be girl faeries, wearing tiny yellow dresses resembling upside down daffodils. Their sparkling buckled shoes shimmered in the glow of their brightly lit dazzling orange wings that shone in the darkness.

The faery-like creatures chattered and hummed in a beautiful tone, enchanting Eddie. He was so engaged in inspecting these exotic beings he didn't even notice the sharp rock underfoot and tripped and fell, twisting his ankle and cutting his foot on the rock as he landed with a thud on the forest floor.

As Eddie fell flat on the ground, hurting himself quite badly in the process, the hypnotic firefly creatures laughed loudly, their cackling tone shaking Eddie up even more. He looked up at them more closely, but too late realised the creatures were transforming in front of his eyes. They weren't beautiful at all; they were actually quite nasty.

Quite suddenly something in them shifted. They turned to face Eddie square on as they bared their sharp teeth in unison, staring at him aggressively, their eyes flashing a bright red. They started making a high-pitched buzzing noise, like a hive of angry bees, as together they formed themselves into a flying dart-shaped group.

Then all at once and very fast, they flew down and attacked Eddie's head as he lay bleeding on the ground.

Melody, who had been concentrating on the path ahead, noticed the negative energy shift and recognised the danger in the faeries hostile behaviour just in time. Her eyes darted around quickly, searching for something to use as a shield. She saw a large leathery palm leaf on the ground and grabbed it as she rushed to Eddie's side, where she used it to shield Eddie's head from the violent attack by these horrid Jekyll-and-Hyde creatures.

How could they have transformed so quickly? From beautiful, etherial faeries one minute to gnashing vampire-like hunters focusing on Eddie as if he was their prey the next? It was really scary and very confusing; nothing was as it first appeared here.

How could they feel safe in this strange land if they couldn't trust what they saw with their own eyes?

Melody's quick thinking and practical nature saved the day for Eddie as most of the loathsome faeries flew off in a hurry once they realised there was nothing to be gained. But one of them was not going to be outdone and while Melody was busy rescuing Eddie, the despicable vampire faery flew behind the palm leaf and angrily took a bite out of Melody's ear.

"Owwwww!" Melody squealed as the needle-like teeth chomped deeply into her ear. As blood rushed from her ear she felt instantly light-headed and wondered how things had escalated so quickly.

They had felt such uplifting lightness when they arrived in Andalustria, and now both were wounded and shocked by what had occurred, particularly Eddie, who lay on the ground with a cut foot and twisted ankle, unable to move far at all. The heart-warming feelings they had experienced from their meeting with Ling evaporated as this unexpected and challenging incident unfolded before their eyes.

As they sat on the ground, using the moist moss from underfoot to clean and soothe their wounds, it occurred to Melody that sometimes things that appear beautiful and mesmerizing can actually be dangerous and bad for you, like the vampire faeries. But sometimes things that appeared ugly and fearsome on the surface may actually be kind and good for you, like Ling.

"You can never judge what's good for you just from what you see on the surface," she muttered. What a thought-provoking journey it was turning out to be for Melody Mind, who loved discovering how things fitted together in the scheme of things to help you solve some of life's challenges.

She knew the wisdom she was learning here in Andalustria would be helpful in many areas of her life when she got home if she could only remember this in future. But here in the present her head was starting to feel even lighter, fuzzy even, as the poison from the vampire faery's bite started to take effect.

"What are we going to do now? You can't walk on your twisted ankle and my ear is still bleeding and hurts like mad, even though I've been holding the moss on it for ages," Melody said in a shaky voice.

"It will be okay Melody, things always work out in the end, you know that, and they will this time." Eddie said, a bit of trepidation in his voice. He did his best to bolster Melody, even though he wasn't at all confident in what he was saying.

They could still see the flickering light and the smoke in the distance; maybe if they called out someone would come to help them. But what if who or what they met was like the vampire faeries? That would be terrible.

How could they tell who was a friend and who was their enemy? It was so hard to know if something was good or bad just from what it looked like, they realised.

Both felt worried and anxious as they wondered what to do next.

Maybe they could find somewhere to rest; they needed something to stop their wounds from bleeding, especially Melody. The wound on her ear was hurting a lot and she told Eddie she wasn't only feeling really light-headed now, her vision was blurring even more, and she felt weak.

Eddie felt agitated and angry, he wasn't used to being immobile and he was getting very worried about Melody. He was Eddie Motion and he was used to moving around and being in the flow and just getting on with things.

But he didn't have a choice. He had to stop and be still or it really hurt his ankle and who knows what damage he would do. If he moved around too much the blood flowing from his wounded foot oozed out more and made him feel quite dizzy too.

They knew their situation was bad, but they didn't really know what to do to make things better, which was a first for both of them.

Melody's vison was really fuzzy now and she couldn't focus at all, which really frightened her. Usually she could easily come up with solutions when there were problems that needed fixing, whether it was a math equation or something to help someone else, she was good at finding answers. But she needed to be able to think and use her mind to focus so she could make that happen, and right now she couldn't do either.

Melody and Eddie realised their natural gifts of thinking and problem-solving and moving and feeling were not going to work for them here.

Or were they?

Chapter 7

Wounded in The Woods

"Crikey! What're we going to do?" Eddie said out loud, putting his hand over his mouth the minute he'd said it, not wanting to scare Melody even more.

Their gifts were rendered useless. All they could do was cuddle together to keep each other warm as they held hands and hoped something would change for the better and improve their situation.

When Eddie wasn't in his natural flow, all the fearful feelings started to surface and overwhelm him. The same thing was happening for Melody. They both sat frozen on the spot for what seemed like an eternity.

They were scared and they could barely see ahead of them at all now, as it was getting darker by the minute. Their young bodies were throbbing and racked with pain due to their injuries. Damp from the cold ground seeped into their bodies, and an icy wind blew up around them making them shiver and tremble.

Feeling extremely sorry for themselves, neither had any idea what was going to happen to them in this strange place. They felt abandoned by their natural gifts at a time when they both really needed them.

Melody drifted in and out of consciousness, which really concerned Eddie, so he kept shaking her to keep her awake. Somehow he knew that if she drifted off completely she might never come back to him.

The nasty bite on her ear had turned a dark blue and a very smelly sort of pus was oozing out of the wound, dripping down the side of her face and onto her shoulder.

Eddie felt tears in the corners of his eyes as his anxiety rose to the surface and the very real terror of their situation began to sink in. What was going to happen to them? Surely this wasn't the end, surely they weren't going to die here in the woods?

He'd never thought dying at such a young age was even a possibility. Eddie had always lived life at full throttle, embracing whatever came his way in such an alive and open-hearted way. He had seen what happened when creatures died so he knew that everyone went back into the earth in the end. He knew it was a natural part of life when someone's time was up. But surely it couldn't be his time just yet? Surely it wasn't Melody's either?

Their situation was drastic and he didn't know how to make it better or how to save them.

How could it have gotten this bad?

It was his fault. He had wanted to come here to discover how to help his mother. Now it looked like a real possibility that they could die right here in this damp, dark place. No one even knew they were here.

Eddie always wanted to help people so he told them the things he knew, so they could make their lives better if they chose to, but how could he help them now?

How could he help anyone when he couldn't even help himself?

Eddie sat on the icy, damp forest floor, sobbing and releasing the pent-up emotions that had built up over the last couple of hours. As he did this his mind started to clear and he didn't feel quite as overwhelmed.

He started remembering how his instinctive know-how had helped him and his friends in the past and had even helped him at school earlier in the day.

Wiping the warm tears from his eyes, Eddie took a very deep breath and decided he'd give his Press Pause recovery formula a go. He figured he had nothing to lose, and it gave him something to do instead of sitting there feeling powerless and sorry for himself.

He knew it wouldn't heal his ankle, but it would help him feel less scared as he acknowledged and moved his emotions, helping them to flow out of his body instead of building up and fogging his mind and his thinking.

He'd always been good at releasing pent-up emotions by acknowledging them and letting them go through his breath so they didn't negatively impact him. But now he wasn't sure what he believed, with all that had happened he felt topsy-turvy.

Eddie could hardly move and had to remain still due to his injury. He felt as if he couldn't take charge of himself as he usually did, which really frightened him.

What had happened earlier at school had caused a combination of sensory overload from all that was going on, as Eddie was such a sponge to others' emotions, the terror of the other children and the shock from the blasting bell and siren sounds that seemed to go on forever had rocked him to his core.

The failure of the adults to take charge of the situation or reassure the children had added to the pressure. Eddie's nervous and emotional system circuitry had overloaded, much like a plug blowing a fuse when it's not grounded.

It had really shocked him that he had "blown a fuse" at school. So although Melody had pulled him through the incident using his Press Pause formula with her touch, grounding his body and using breathing to reconnect him, it made him doubt himself now.

This felt like a life-or-death situation and he had lost a lot of his usual confidence after the vampire faeries had tricked him. Could he really trust himself and his abilities?

No time for doubt now, he realised, it was his turn to look after Melody as she was fading fast. He knew he had to try even if he doubted himself, as he knew how damaging doubting yourself can be. He had seen how it had sapped his mother's energy and stolen her vibrancy. He wasn't going to let that happen to him.

After all, that was why he was here, to help his mother to find answers so she could re-discover her magik. But how could he do that if he couldn't even help himself or Melody?

"Okay, Eddie remember what works," he said out loud, encouraging himself to bolster his confidence.

"It's no good pushing my feelings and emotions away, nor pretending I don't have any and just get on with it, like a big tough guy. If I push my feelings down into my body they'll only pop up another time when I don't expect them to and bite me in the bum. Or the feeling will fester inside me like the sore on Melody's ear, creating poison in my mind that will make me think bad things about myself," Eddie said out loud, trying to increase his courage.

He knew he had to express and release his feelings if he was ever going to find a way through the terrible situation they were in now.

Wasn't life strange. One minute you think you know a lot, have a lot of wisdom and are skipping along just fine, having fun. Then something unexpected happens that can quickly turn things around to make it even better, or make it a whole lot worse. And you never know which way it's going to go, he thought as he rallied himself.

One thing was for certain, life was continually changing and shifting, so it was really important to know how to create your own inner foundation of safety no matter what happens. Then it's easier to deal with and overcome the challenges life sends, because you know deep down that *you're the only one* who can truly take charge of how you manage yourself in any situation. Eddie knew this deep inside; now he just had to do it here.

Right, he needed to identify and release his emotions as he knew his mind would become clearer once he did that. Then he could work out what to do and not just drown in self-doubt and self-pity or make himself bullet-proof and close off his heart.

Time for Eddie to Press Pause, he thought. Although one hand was supporting him to sit upright, the other arm was protectively around Melody. But he knew he needed to put his hand on his body so he could get back in touch with his body.

Gently he lowered Melody onto the mossy pillow he made for her head and covered her up with his school jumper so she didn't get colder.

Tangible Magik Press Pause Formula (part 1)

Eddie put his hand on his stomach, then he did the following:

- breathed in deeply through his nose, breathing right down to his stomach.

- pushed his stomach out with the air that flowed into his body from his breath.

- held his breath in his stomach as he counted to three in his head.

- blew his breath out through his mouth with a big *whoosh* sound.

- then released the tense emotions out of his breath that he'd been tightly holding onto.

Eddie felt tears rush down his face again as he breathed out and released the fear and worry of this extraordinary day. He let himself cry and allowed his feelings to flow out of his body because he knew, even though it was hard right now, doing this was really good for him and he'd soon feel much better once he released the tension from his body.

The tears stopped flowing as he let go. He felt angry as heat flushed across his face, making his cheeks glow bright red. He felt angry with the vampire faeries for biting Melody, angry with his school teacher for not taking control of the situation to make them feel safe. And he was really angry that he'd been tricked by the faeries mesmerizing, scheming behaviour. He felt really silly and embarrassed about that.

If only he hadn't been enchanted by their beauty none of this would have happened. He would have seen the sharp rock on the ground, as he was usually good at noticing things like that. Above all, if he hadn't been so silly Melody, his best friend, wouldn't be hurt and dangerously close to fading away as she lay on the forest floor.

Eddie thought he really was very stupid. Then he realised that, most of all, he was angry with himself.

As he acknowledged and released his emotions he continued breathing deeply into his body. The feelings flowed around and out of his body as he breathed them out with the tears and the rage. He felt the storm of built-up emotions gradually pass, as it was replaced with a quiet stillness that made him feel quite peaceful.

He kept breathing in and out, releasing and calming himself, as his natural faith started to return.

Eddie knew he needed to completely accept himself and the situation if he wanted his wisdom to return so he could figure out what to do. The wisdom couldn't work if he fought against accepting it or resisted the situation.

He knew he needed to forgive himself for the normal human weakness of being captivated by something that appeared beautiful, even though it was only an illusion.

He needed to be his own best friend right now!

Eddie Motion was wise beyond his years. He had a deep knowing from days gone by, a knowing that he had been born with. He knew that when he was connected with himself his life flowed easily. He knew that when he was in the flow of life, celebrating his strengths and taking responsibility to own and work on his weaknesses and loving himself for both, then things just worked out.

He knew that when he did the same for other people and let go of judging himself or anyone else, life was great. That was the true magik he had, and his mother used to have it, too. It was a deep knowing, a deep understanding of how to work *with life* in order to experience the joy and power that was possible in each moment.

Yes, that was his purpose, he was here to help his mother, but maybe he was here to remember and fully own his own wisdom, too. "There's a thought," Eddie smiled to himself.

"I'm starting to think a bit like Melody. I suppose that's what happens when you appreciate and care about each other, you end up sharing each other's gifts. Wow, that's cool," he said out loud.

The realisations came to him as he released the last of his stored-up emotions and finished off his Press Pause formula. This is how Eddie ensured he was where he needed to be within himself so he could create the changes that needed to happen.

Tangible Magik Press Pause Formula (part 2)
Eddie continued to hold his hand on his stomach and did the following:

- imagined a time when he felt completely safe and happy (for him it was running through the meadow close to home with his faithful dog, Missy).

- took another deep breath in through his nose, right down to his stomach.

- filled his whole body with the sense of safety and comfort from his memories.

- breathed out through his mouth, releasing any remaining feelings he didn't want.

- released his fear, worry, anger and sadness

- just blowing all the feelings he didn't want right out of his body with every exhale.

Eddie felt the formula working as his energy rose and his spirits lifted.

He knew he needed to add something extra to his formula this time around, though.

- "I forgive you, Eddie Motion, for being tricked by things that appeared beautiful on the surface, but weren't beautiful at all, just plain dangerous," he said to himself.

- "I forgive you, Eddie Motion, for being human." He repeated the statements three times.

- Then he took three more deep breaths and placed both his hands on the ground.

Eddie had shut his eyes so he could concentrate and bring his energy back. Now he gradually opened his eyes, rubbing them as they started to clear.

Suddenly he became aware of a large shape in front of him. He rubbed his eyes again; wanting to be sure he wasn't seeing things. No he wasn't imagining it; a tall man in long dark robes stood in front of him.

Oh my! Now what?

Chapter 8
Aaron Shows The Way

The tall man looked down at Eddie and across at Melody, who by now was lying semi-conscious on the ground. He smiled, the smile of "knowing" that offered wisdom as only a wise man could.

His smile would light up a thousand lightbulbs with its brightness and warm the hearts of a nation with the love that was delivered with it. Eddie knew they had been rescued, everything would be all right now. This man in front of him was very familiar; he knew this man, even though he'd never met him before.

Or had he? Somehow he knew him!

"My name is Aaron. It looks like you could do with some help, young man, let's get you sorted," he offered.

Aaron was very tall, maybe seven or eight feet, with long, grey, wavy hair that flowed down over his shoulders and beyond. From where Eddie sat on the ground it was hard to tell where, or if, the hair ended. He had deep brown eyes that melted into you and made you feel as if he knew all about you, just by looking at you. It felt as if he saw into your soul and said, "Welcome Home," as he embraced you with his gaze.

Eddie felt a huge sense of relief. He knew they were safe, whether it was his magical formulas that had helped him draw the feeling of safety into his own body, or perhaps Chandor the Raven had shown Aaron where they were? Perhaps it was the alchemy that occurred in this land that had brought this wonderful, biblical-looking person to arrive before him. Eddie didn't really care. He was just relieved to finally feel safe.

He was so grateful to see Aaron, the one he somehow knew from long ago.

"My dear child, you have done well," said the gentle, mystical man.

"You have gone through a lot today, what with blowing fuses and learning lessons from ugly creatures who aren't ugly at all, and being attacked by beautiful, mesmerizing creatures who aren't really beautiful at all. Then being lost and wounded, alone and afraid in the forest. Yet you found the courage to evoke your own deep wisdom, so you could release what no longer served you and reconnect back to yourself in such a powerful way. We are very proud of you, young man, and we thank you for coming to see us in Andalustria. Now we can remind you who you are, so you can help your mother remember who she is, too. Then you can both come home to feel truly safe to be who you are both meant to be out in the world."

Eddie realised Aaron kept saying "We," but he could only see Aaron so who was the "We," he wondered?

What was he talking about – "remember who he was," – Eddie wondered as his ears pricked up when his mother was mentioned, for he believed helping his mother was the whole reason he was here in Andalustria.

"Can you fix Melody, please?" Eddie asked as he pulled himself together. "Those horrid vampire faeries attacked her when she was defending me and her ear's really bad, it's turned totally blue." Eddie squealed in a high-pitched voice that he didn't even recognise as his own.

"It's all in hand dear boy, now we must let the Squiggins look after you both. You have done your bit by using your techniques, now just relax and let them do their work."

Aaron's deep melodic tone and his words felt as comforting as a cup of warm hot chocolate on a cold winter's night.

Eddie watched with great interest as a very curious group of creatures scurried along the ground and climbed all over Melody. They could only be described as a tribe of mice at first glance. They carried large, strangely shaped purple-spotted mushrooms, which they placed in their mouths, swirling them round and round until they transformed the mushrooms into some sort of gooey paste they plastered all over Melody's ear.

Eddie looked closer and realised that they weren't actually mice at all. They had mice legs and long mice tails, but gnome-like heads of both men and women. They were a vibrant and jolly bunch with their vividly coloured hats, matching gloves and tiny black patent-leather shoes with shiny buckles on their incredibly tiny feet.

Each of the Squiggins had their own unique style and colour co-ordination. Despite all Eddie had recently been through he couldn't help but smile at the sight of these industrious creatures helping heal Melody.

What an interesting place Andalustria was, nothing was actually what it appeared to be at first glance, and he realised now that was all okay.

One of the Squiggins looked up at Eddie, gestured his head towards Eddie's ankle and raised his thumb in a "thumbs up, okay" gesture. Eddie took this to mean, "Was it okay to sort out the cut on his foot and his twisted ankle?"

Eddie nodded, smiled at the little blended creature standing by his feet and gave him a thumbs-up gesture back. The little creature leapt right up onto Eddie's shoulder and started shouting directions to the other Squiggins to get to work on Eddie's injuries.

Eddie didn't understand their language, although somehow he knew he would at some point. He lay back and let them work on him, feeling a sense of relief and calm wash over him.

The Squiggins used the same purple-mushroom process on Eddie's cut foot as they had with Melody's ear. Eddie stared in wonder as the creatures whizzed around faster and faster until they created a deep basin like hole in the ground. Then they dashed around and around at racing car speed, mixing the orange clay-like earth with a silver powder they poured into the earth from out of their hats. They continued racing around and around until a thick paste was formed.

The Squiggins rallied around and placed the paste like a poultice around Eddie's ankle, on top of the purple mushroom gooey substance. It felt cool to the touch and instantly soothed the throbbing pain that had been building up in his whole body.

As Eddie lay back, the Squiggin standing on his shoulder giving orders jumped up above his head and started flying around in circles, changing into a completely different form as he did so.

The Squiggin transformed before Eddie's eyes, becoming silver in colour from top to toe and a totally different creature that no longer resembled a Squiggin at all. Like most things in this new land, the creature appeared to be a blend of several different aspects. He was a solid silver faery, elfin-like figure, but also looked a bit like a mini Viking God with wings.

Eddie had learnt about Viking Gods at school and this small flying creature definitely looked like a mini version of one of them as it transformed before his eyes.

The creature turned to him and said in words Eddie could actually understand, "I am Erik, and I'm your sprite. I have always been with you, bringing lightness, fun, and joy into your life. I watch over you and bring lightness in when darkness and sadness is present."

With this Erik flew up in the air with his freshly sprouted wings and circled seven times around Eddie's ankle and foot with incredible speed, creating a heat in Eddie's ankle that flowed into his foot and all the way up his body.

Eddie suddenly found himself laughing and crying with happiness all at the same time as he realised that, just as with Aaron, somehow he knew Erik. He had seen him many times in many forms in his mind's eye. He knew this silver mini-God, and he loved him in an instant.

Erik hovered back toward Eddie's head and said, "I'm always with you Eddie, I am your lifetime sprite. You can call on me any time you want to bring in fun, lightness, and add a sparkle to life. Even if you don't see me, you know I am always with you now. I can take on any form, but how you see me now is my natural form," Erik explained, running his hands down his silver body.

"Don't be surprised if I appear different when we meet again, as I blend in as is needed for each situation to create the most beneficial outcome for you, my friend."

With that, Erik flew off, followed by most of his Squiggin helpers as they headed into the forest. All left except one Squiggin who sat on Melody's shoulder, talking in her ear.

Eddie was relieved to see Melody had now awakened and was sitting upright as the colour slowly returned to her cheeks. She was looking a lot brighter after the Squiggins' treatment. The Squiggin on Melody's shoulder also transformed into a silver sprite similar to Eddie's, except this one looked like a girl.

Eddie guessed this creature was Melody's sprite that was going to watch out for her. *Maybe everyone had sprites, but you could only see them when you came to Andalustria? How cool would it be if everyone had a sprite like Erik that watched out for you,* Eddie thought.

Melody was now wide awake. Her eyes shone brightly and she looked a lot better, thank goodness. Eddie was really happy to see that Melody's ear had returned to its usual human pink colour now. The dark-blue smelly goo had disappeared altogether.

"Thank you," she said as she looked over and smiled at Eddie.

"Thank me for what? You saved me after I blew a fuse, Melody, you're my hero!"

"Thank you, but I helped you using *your tangible magik*. If you hadn't shown me how to do it, I wouldn't have known what to do at all. Now you're showing me your world here in Andalustria. This is such an incredible land of adventure, new knowledge and enchantment. It's really helping me see that wavy lines are just as important as straight lines. I can never thank you enough for that Eddie, as it's really opened my mind."

Melody's face lit up as she added, "And I've even discovered I have my very own sprite!"

Eddie thought for a moment and then asked, "Melody, what do you mean *'my world?'*"

"This has all happened because you wanted to help your mother. You created this world to show you the way; without you we wouldn't be here at all," Melody explained.

Eddie sat bolt upright. "I never looked at it like that, I suppose you might have a point. But Aaron was already here, he's been here for thousands of years. These are all ancient creatures and beings of the world that have been around far longer than we could ever count," he said to Melody.

"Yes, Eddie, I do believe that's true. But how could you know that, if it wasn't *your* world too?"

The strength of emotion that coursed through Eddie at Melody's acknowledgment threatened tears, but he didn't really know why he felt so moved.

As was his way, he sat with his feelings, letting them ebb and flow. He pressed pause and breathed into his body and through his emotions. There was no bottling feelings and thoughts up for Eddie, he allowed everything to flow through him until he felt calm and relaxed.

He couldn't explain it yet but he knew deep within him that what Melody said was true. He didn't know why or how but in some funny way he had come home.

In trying to help his mother find her magik, he was rediscovering that he, too, was magikal, that his notions, formulas and insights along with his instinctive wisdom was truly valuable. It had already saved both of them several times in one way or another, and that was just today.

Today had indeed been an extraordinary day! Eddie knew deep in his heart and soul that even if he did come from this place, right now he was only a visitor. Whatever he discovered here, he would take home to his world to help children and adults there in his own special way.

Eddie looked down at his foot and saw it had completely healed. There wasn't a mark or even the tiniest sign that he'd cut his foot or had an injury at all.

Aaron gestured for him to stand and he tentatively got to his feet, still a bit worried it might hurt as it had before. Thanks to Erik and the team of Squiggins there was no pain at all, not even a twinge. He felt like his old self again.

As he straightened his clothes and tidied himself up after lying on the forest floor for so long, a thought crossed his mind. *Why had it taken so long for Aaron and Erik to rescue them when they were obviously very wise, mystical creatures that seemed to be able to travel around this world very quickly?*

Why hadn't Chandor the Raven protected them so they didn't get hurt in the first place? Perhaps he should ask Aaron.

He didn't want to be ungrateful when they'd just been rescued, but he'd like to know as it seemed strange that they had needed to go through so much, even feeling they could die at one point, before they were rescued.

Maybe it could all have been avoided if the raven had protected them as the Zingledibod tree said he was supposed to do. And now the raven was nowhere in sight, which was odd and really quite annoying.

"Eddie, there's no point wondering and worrying. If you've got something to ask you need to have the courage to ask, rather than brewing on your thoughts and feeling like a boiling kettle on an open fire," Aaron encouraged.

Eddie was usually very open and readily asked questions, but he felt a bit silly and ungrateful, as Aaron had probably just saved their lives. But the thoughts niggled away at him and Aaron seemed to be able to read his mind anyway, so he might as well ask the question. He was starting to feel quite annoyed, and he didn't like that feeling.

Aaron had read Eddie's thoughts and knew what was on his mind, but he knew it was important that Eddie tell him how he was feeling, rather than keep it bottled up inside him. So he sat down on the nearest rock and encouraged Eddie to go ahead and speak.

"Come along, tell us what's on your mind. It's important to have the courage to talk about and express your feelings, because if you don't say anything and keep things locked up inside you, you'll get sick, and we can't have that, can we? You have been very brave today and faced a lot. Now you need to have the courage to speak up and tell me how you feel."

"Courage comes in many forms Eddie," Aaron said. "At times you need to be brave and have the courage to take action. At other times it's important to use your courage to be still and calm. Sometimes you need to have the courage to be quiet, to listen and observe. You also need to have the courage to admit when you are wrong and take responsibility, as well as the courage to stand up for what is right."

"Then there are times like these, where you need to be true to yourself and speak up. But one of the most important acts of bravery is to use your wisdom to know when to do what!" Aaron said with a deep chuckle.

Chapter 9

E-Motion in Action

Eddie felt his face get hotter and redder and redder with embarrassment as his feelings and emotions came bubbling to the surface.

He felt angry, but also relieved that he could say what he'd been thinking as he really didn't want to be angry with Aaron, or any of his new friends. But he did want to know why they had been left for so long to suffer when maybe they could have been rescued earlier.

As his emotions started to release, Eddie steadied himself and put his hand on his stomach again and "Pressed Pause." He blew out a lot of his feelings, then took in large gulps of fresh air, trying to take charge of himself so he could ask Aaron his question.

As he breathed out and let the fresh air enter his body with his breathing formula, all the built-up anger and fear he'd felt about the awful situation they'd been in, along with the relief of being rescued, released from his body. He began to feel better and felt himself calming down.

"Why did it take so long to rescue us?" Eddie blurted out; he hadn't quite calmed himself enough yet to ask the question in a relaxed or polite way.

"I'm sorry you had to go through all those tough experiences, Eddie, and yes, you are right, we could have rescued you earlier," Aaron said.

Eddie could feel his face getting hot again as his anger rose up once more at what Aaron was saying. He carried on breathing deeply and blowing the anger out of his body, managing to calm himself enough to actually hear the next thing Aaron said, which made all the difference as to how he would feel about things.

"You came to this world to help your mother, which is admirable, Eddie," Aaron said. "However, the deeper purpose for you coming here was to grow *your* confidence muscle and reclaim *your own* magik. You need to develop greater resilience so you can use the tangible magik to full effect in your world. Then, and only then, can you harness the wisdom fully, as that is your true path.

"It is only when we have challenges and adversity in life that we can truly test what we are made, of so we can develop and strengthen our skills and gifts," Aaron said.

"Everyone needs to experience trials in life, as working through them helps build our confidence and self-belief. It also enables us to experience a greater sense of achievement through knowing we can overcome difficulties that occur in our life at times. When things are too easy, and you don't experience any challenges, then you never get the opportunity to discover who you truly are, nor do you develop into who you are meant to be.

"That doesn't mean you have to have problems all the time," Aaron continued, "but working toward something and growing your own life muscles is really important if you want to live a truly satisfying and happy life. Right now it may feel unfair that you had to suffer, when you could have been rescued sooner. But take a moment to think about it Eddie: what did you learn by experiencing that challenge? What did you discover about your formulas? What did you uncover about yourself?"

Smiling, he added, "Do you feel different than you did before?"

By now Eddie had calmed down and was able to truly listen and absorb what Aaron said. He considered Aaron's questions, as did Melody who had been sitting quietly, watching this very interesting exchange between Aaron and her best friend.

"I think I get your point," Eddie began. "I know my 'Press Pause Tangible Magik' formula really works now, even in the toughest situations. That does give me more faith in how valuable it is – more than before. And I do feel as if something in me has changed. My feelings have relaxed as I released the intensity. I feel stronger somehow, as if I've been through a battle and won," Eddie said.

"Well you have come through a battle, what you thought at one point might be a life-threatening fight," Aaron replied.

"You've also come through a battle over your thoughts and emotions. You took charge of yourself so they didn't totally take over, overpowering and rendering you helpless. Everyone can be overwhelmed at times. And now you have the courage to work through this challenge by choosing how to deal with a situation. You have chosen to take charge of your emotions, even when they threatened to overcome you, so that you could express your feelings in a positive way. This allowed you to be honest with yourself and with me, so we could talk through a problem that may have got in the way of us being the very best of friends.

"You have indeed grown many wonderful muscles from this experience, Eddie." "Even though it was very hard for you and Melody to go through all that, can you see how valuable this experience has been for you both?"

Both Eddie and Melody felt a warm glow as they recognised the truth in the words Aaron spoke. They realised their experiences had indeed made them stronger and wiser in many ways and they had grown muscles they never would have thought possible nor needed.

Eddie remembered his mother telling him the story about the butterfly when he wanted to help the caterpillar out of its cocoon, so it didn't have to struggle so hard to transform into a butterfly.

His mother had told him it was because the butterfly had to struggle by pushing its wings against the walls of the cocoon so that it could strengthen its developing wings. She told Eddie that if he cut the cocoon open to set the butterfly free, even if he was trying to help, the butterfly wouldn't be able to develop the strength it needed in its wings in order to fly and be able to survive.

Eddie understood now. If Aaron had rushed to rescue him straight away he wouldn't have been able to develop his strength to know how to survive in difficult situations. This knowledge would now serve him well for the rest of his life.

"Hmmmm," Eddie said loudly, "so people who are just given things for doing nothing never get the chance to develop themselves fully, nor get to experience the sense of real achievement, or what feels to me right now like a happiness that comes from the inside out."

Who would have thought he could feel so good, considering his feelings only a few minutes ago, before he truly understood what he had been through and the value of this lesson. Maybe he could tell other people about this once he got back to his world, as he realised this was probably a very important lesson for everyone. He hoped they didn't need to experience a life-threatening situation to learn it.

"You've got it, Eddie," Aaron said, patting him on the back.

"Now we must get on our way," Aaron said, tapping his long wooden staff on the ground three times. The ground rumbled as a deep hush fell over the forest of knightly trees. A light shone brightly way ahead, beckoning them onward. Aaron gestured for Eddie and Melody to follow him as he set off toward the glowing light.

They travelled quickly along the path, noticing the gently gurgling stream flowing beside them as they continued their journey once again to who knew where.

Their feet seemed to hardly touch the ground. Even though they knew they were walking, it was as if they were floating along the earth path at a much greater speed than was humanly possible. But as Eddie and

Melody were beginning to realise, anything was possible in this new land of discovery and rediscovery.

Two flashes of silver whizzed past either side of Eddie and Melody. Although they didn't see more than a flash, both knew they were their sprites.

Eddie already felt a strong connection to his sprite. His mind was clearing as if he'd been asleep in a deep fog and he now realised Erik had shown up in many forms throughout his life to support him in one way or another. Eddie felt immense gratitude that he was now fully aware of Erik's presence in his life.

I must ask Melody the name of her sprite, he thought as they float-walked along the path.

How exhilarating, terrifying and heart-warming it was to be part of this new world. Or was it an old world they were just revisiting? Eddie just didn't know.

Time seemed unimportant here. Maybe he was centuries old like Aaron and he and Melody had been together in many lifetimes? It didn't matter in the big scheme of things but it was "interesting" as Melody would say. Both knew they were exactly where they needed to be right now and it felt good being on this journey together as they uncovered new and maybe even forever friends along the way.

The forest became even darker as nightfall drew upon them. A colony of small creatures glowing a vibrant blue appeared, flying around them all. The creatures exuded a smell just like the old-fashioned roses in Eddie's grandmother's garden, making everyone feel cosy and safe.

He couldn't tell what they actually looked like, as the glowing blue was just too shiny to see anything except a blue translucent glow. After his last mishap with the vampire faeries he was determined he wasn't going to be drawn in or tricked by these creatures as he had been before.

The blue flying creatures lit the way as they flew in unison alongside and ahead of them, allowing them all to see the path and the surrounding area very clearly even though it was almost pitch black now.

"What are these blue creatures? Are they friendly, or are they dangerous like the vampire faeries?" Eddie asked Aaron.

"They are the Devas and guardians of this forest, Eddie. They are our friends and have chosen to help us tonight by lighting the way ahead," Aaron responded. "Every place in nature has Devas that act as guardians of that domain. Some will choose to work with you and some will choose to test you to see if you have the courage to grow and be trusted by them," he explained.

"The vampire faeries are neither good nor bad. They are there to remind you to be mindful not to be led by your first attraction to something and to check it out and question it, before diving in and following blindly down a certain path.

"They are there for a reason and serve a very valuable purpose to help you learn, so they actually help you too," Aaron explained.

Eddie understood what Aaron said on one level, but he struggled to feel grateful towards the vampire faeries right now, after recently experiencing the distress of their attack and the pain from their injuries. But maybe that would come. Who knew in this land where things were never what they appeared at first sight?

He understood that it wasn't all the vampire faeries fault that they had been injured. He realised he was responsible for being taken in by their apparent beauty and not keeping his attention on the path ahead. That wasn't their fault; he was the only one responsible for that and he had to own his part. So what Aaron said did make sense, he reasoned, and as he worked through it he stopped feeling quite so angry toward the vampire faeries.

Eddie discussed his revelations about the vampire faeries with Melody and she realised that one of the most wonderful things about Eddie was his ability to take responsibility for his part in whatever occurred, as well as recognising where it was not his responsibility.

Eddie felt his emotions of anger, fear, sadness, and all the myriad of feelings that all human beings feel. But because he used his empowering formulas to let his emotions flow through him, rather than holding onto them, he could see where he could change how he felt by taking responsibility for his feelings and his actions whenever something occurred.

This made Eddie very strong and powerful, Melody reasoned, as he didn't spend time blaming other people, or giving his power away to anything outside of himself, nor worry about things that were out of his control that he couldn't change. Eddie worked out what he needed to take responsibility for and owned it, then let his emotions flow and took charge so he learned from the experience.

Melody thought this was one of the very best qualities Eddie had, and one he was very good at, as it allowed him to take charge of what happened in his life quickly and in a very positive way. That was why even though Eddie was more sensitive than most boys appeared to be, no one ever teased or bullied him because he cared for people in such a deep way. And due to his natural instincts, in addition to reading the language of people, he knew how people really felt without them even saying a word.

Owning his own stuff meant Eddie didn't dump his feelings onto others or blame them for things that weren't actually theirs. People not only liked him for that, they thought he was very strong and brave, for he often stood up for people who couldn't stand up for themselves, but in a really positive way that empowered them to grow strength in themselves.

Of course, Eddie was completely unaware of how amazing he was to have all these wonderful gifts that not only helped him, but helped so many people in small and large ways all the time. He suffered the same self-doubt, anxiety, and worry that everyone else did. The difference was Eddie knew he was feeling something and he didn't hide it from himself; instead he used his formulas to quickly turn things around.

Melody thought she must really write down what they'd discovered in Andalustria, as well as Eddie's insights and formulas, as she had started doing earlier at school. She knew how well and how quickly Eddie's techniques worked. She knew with all her heart that they would make life easier for other children and probably some adults, too. So their lives would be happier and a lot more magikal!

Chapter 10

The Healing waters of Nardor

A wave of exhaustion washed over Eddie and Melody as they walked together deep in thought about the journey they were on. The sky was dark, and they had no idea of time or how long they'd been in Andalustria. Night and day were different here and the bone-tired weariness from all the events they had experienced so far descended upon them.

Aaron reached under his travel-worn robes, pulling what looked like a large circular piece of bright orange Turkish bread from the depths of his clothing. He ripped it in two, handing them each a piece. "The Levanos will replenish your energy and sustain you as we continue our journey" he said. "It grows deep in the forest and is filled with the wholesome goodness of the earth. It will provide the balance of energy that you need. Eat up, it's good" said Aaron, his eyes twinkling.

Neither of them had thought about food, having been so engrossed with all that had happened. But they now realised how hungry they were as the garlicy, cheesy aroma wafted from the warm Levanos, making their mouths water; they snatched hungrily at the bread as Aaron offered it to them.

It smelled so good, but how could it be warm? Did Aaron have an oven under his robes, Melody wondered? As hunger overtook her enquiring mind she decided it didn't really matter and ravenously devoured the nourishing food.

Eddie enjoyed the texture of the Levanos, it was crunchy on the outside and warm and doughy on the inside like freshly baked bread, yet it felt light as air in your mouth and was easily soaked up by his aching body, it made him feel energized and refreshed just as if he were eating a big portion of fresh fruit and vegetables.

As they walked along munching on the Levanos, revitalizing energy flooded their tired bodies and after only a couple of mouthfuls they felt full. Completely contented, they looked gratefully at Aaron, their rescuer. This kindly wise man was teaching them so much as he led them across this land.

As they relaxed, they noticed the path ahead as it steered them toward a lush oasis that opened out in front of them. A hollow within the verdant glen revealed a luminous blue shimmering lake dipping gracefully into the earth; as the squidgy vegetation underfoot gently held their weight like a delicate hand, they made their way in wonder toward the lake.

"It's beautiful!" said Melody surveying the glade, "it's the complete opposite of the forest. It's so bright and colourful, the air crackles and sparkles as if it's jumping for joy!"

Eddie quickly snapped out of his reverie, looking up to see what Melody was getting so excited about, as it was most unlike her.

As Eddie raised his head, one of the blue Devas flew in front of him at eye level. Hovering just above his nose, it chuckled to itself; the beautiful shiny creature slowly turned around so its back was towards Eddie. Then it did something completely unexpected – it flashed and wiggled its vibrant blue bottom back and forth at Eddie and swiftly zipped off into the distance chuckling away. This was quickly followed by Erik the sprite whizzing past Eddie's head, his iridescent silver-winged body releasing a loud farting, whooshing-tooting sound that echoed around them as he flew in circles overhead, chortling away with the joy of it all, as only a merry sprite can do.

Eddie nearly jumped out of his skin with all the commotion, his fight or flight reactions kicking in, as the chilling memory of the vampire faeries flashed across his mind. Fear and adrenalin rushed through his body. His back stiffened, his fists clenched, his breath caught at the top of his chest and he jolted bolt upright in shock, like a startled meerkat on the lookout for predators.

His shock rapidly turned to relief and then embarrassment as he realised what it really was and caught sight of Melody holding her stomach doubled over with uncontrollable laughter as she witnessed his reaction to the cheeky Deva's behaviour. Aaron guffawed loudly, emitting a deep roar as he watched the fun and merriment play out in front of him.

Eddie's body quickly relaxed, his knees buckling beneath him as he caught Melody's contagious laughter, giving way to a fit of the giggles himself as much in relief as anything else.

Eddie realised how silly he must have looked as the farting sprite and blue bottom flashing Deva continued flying round them emitting even louder noises, encouraged by the uplifting effect they saw it was having on everyone.

He saw the funny side of the Deva's mischievous antics, made even more amusing by the fact that as sacred, revered guardians of the forest they weren't expected to behave in this amusing, light-hearted way. Maybe he was wrong; just because they were wise important creatures that held the balance of the forest, didn't have to mean that the Devas didn't have any fun. "Hummm," he wondered; if that applied to other people who had important things to do, wouldn't it be great if they also allowed themselves to have fun and relax too? *"Wouldn't that be wonderful, it would certainly change some things in his world?"* he pondered.

As they all recovered their equilibrium they noticed how the landscape around them was changing. They had stepped into what felt like a cavernous cocoon, a valley that drew them ever onward toward a magnificent waterfall of luminescent blue water cascading down into an inviting, silken pool. The azure, turquoise blues and white and silver spray from the waterfall danced joyfully across the lagoon spraying its mist into their faces as they approached this unexpected haven.

The luminescent water hummed and shimmered a wash of synergised colour, its vibrating energy tempting them to join the dance. Neither of them had ever seen anything quite so magnificent before; it was absolutely stunning.

"Go ahead" Aaron said as they looked round at him checking things out. "This is the Nardor Lagoon, it's perfectly safe. In fact these waters will relax your tired muscles and calm your mind after all you've been through," he said.

Melody's ears pricked up when Aaron called what appeared to be a lake, *a lagoon,* she thought lagoons were usually by the sea. But as the shimmering water beckoned, Melody decided to just accept it, rather than keep questioning, which felt very freeing, as things were not always what they appeared here in Andalustria.

Eddie and Melody didn't need to be told twice; throwing off their outer clothes, they jumped into the pulsing water in their underwear and started swimming toward the voluminous waterfall that danced its magik into the lagoon.

The warm water brushed lightly over their skin, giving their bodies a soothing massage as they glided through it. The impetus to rush forward slowly ebbed as the calming water gently stroked their skin as they swam toward the ledge that sat under the waterfall.

Melody floated on her back feeling the tingling comb of flowing water brush lovingly through her hair. As she tilted her head back in the buoyant support of the water she noticed the magenta-blossomed trees stretching over the lagoon, dipping their harvest into the water. The vibrant blooms mirrored their beautiful hues in the blue liquid under the light of the majestic moon that hung above her, creating a purple blue ripple of colour that gleamed its beauty right across the lagoon, stretching its reach all the way to the waterfall like a long finger pointing the way.

Melody was happy just floating along in the beautiful thermal waters, feeling no desire to analyse or think about anything in particular, getting in touch with her senses as she completely relaxed in the calming waters, totally letting go of all cares and worries, something she'd never really done before.

People often felt Melody analysed and thought about things too much and she'd been given all sorts of labels in the past just so people could try to understand how to treat her. But really she was just a sensitive girl whose awareness and intelligence was far beyond most people's comprehension. There was nothing wrong with Melody, she was just different from other people, but she was also learning that she was just the same as everyone else in so many ways as well!

Eddie reached the ledge under the waterfall, after swimming excitedly across the lagoon as tiny rainbow-hued fish gently bumped against his body like a wave of tiny kisses to investigate who had entered their world. He turned to watch Melody floating along and was happy to see his friend so relaxed and peaceful as she enjoyed the healing waters.

As the waterfall's thunderous cascade splashed over him, cleansing and revitalizing his senses, Eddie gripped the edge of the ledge with one hand to steady himself. The sensations from the alternating warm and cold blasts of water that hit his head and rushed down his body made him feel so alive.

He decided to climb up and sit on the ledge but couldn't work out how to get there, as it was pretty slippery with all the water. As he looked around to find somewhere easier to climb up onto the ledge, a fur paw reached down and took his arm.

The fur arm and bearlike paw pulled him up easily onto the ledge and into the opening of the cavern behind the waterfall. Eddie's breath rushed into the top of his chest. Everything happened so fast he didn't get a chance to catch his breath or work out what was going on.

Now, sitting on the ledge under the waterfall, he looked at the creature who had hauled him out of the water and into the cavern. Surprisingly, he wasn't at all frightened, just intrigued as he looked at the furry orange bear-like creature who stood beside him.

It appeared to be a cross between a bear and a monkey, but also resembled something else that he couldn't quite place as it padded around him with its giant orange feet. "That's it!" he said to himself. The creature reminded him of a Sasquatch or "Big Foot" he thought they were called, but a much smaller version.

The creature smiled offering Eddie his hand as it helped him into a standing position. The furry being was about half a head taller than Eddie and was completely covered in long orange hair – or maybe it was fur. It had deep brown eyes that shone and twinkled at Eddie as it smiled at him.

Well, it definitely seemed friendly, Eddie thought.

The creature began talking in a soft melodic tone, which made Eddie immediately relax. It was almost as if it were singing to him, as he felt the friendliness flowing out of the furry creature. The miniature Big Foot spoke to him in a different language, Eddie realised, yet he could understand it in the same way as he had done with Ling.

"Welcome to Nardor Lagoon, my name is Spellbound," the creature said as it leaned forward to hug Eddie. Its warm furry body helped mop up the rapidly cooling water from his body and began to warm him, as Eddie felt the cool draught coming from the cavern behind them.

Spellbound exuded an odd but quite pleasant odour, like a combination of almond marzipan, freshly baked gingerbread, and wet dog fur. Strangely, it felt totally natural for this unusual furry creature to hug him, as Eddie often hugged people, which took them aback when they weren't expecting it.

"Come, warm yourself by the fire," Spellbound said gesturing his outstretched paw further into the cave. As Eddie followed him toward the flickering firelight, he shivered, feeling the dampness of the cave seep into his bones, as his wet underwear clung to his body.

As they headed into the cave the space opened up revealing another smaller waterfall flowing down the back of the cavern, creating its own beautiful luminescent pool of water at its base. The water glowed and shimmered and Eddie noticed that white, turquoise, blue, and rainbow-coloured crystals lined the pool. The water seemed to pulse and vibrate and felt warm to the touch as Eddie reached down to run the shiny liquid through his hands. Just touching the water warmed his whole body, drying his underwear and easing his chills.

High above the waterfall a wide cylindrical cavity opened to expose a very unusual looking sky – much different from the sky outside the cave. As he gazed upward he saw planets, other worlds and a myriad of stars glistening in the splendour of a darkened sky. It was a unique and extremely magikal experience. Eddie was used to Melody pointing out stars and planets as that was her thing but this was completely different; it seemed as if he could see the whole universe up there through the small cavity in the rock.

"I wish Melody was here to see this, she'd absolutely love it," he said out loud to no one in particular.

"Indeed." He recognised Aaron's deep resonant tone straight away without even turning round. "It's incredible!" Melody said, rushing past Aaron completely oblivious of the furry orange Sasquatch-like creature she'd yet to meet. She grabbed Eddie's hand and they stood side by side peering up at the night sky with awe.

Eventually Melody drew a breath, registering where she was. She looked briefly around but her attention was rapidly drawn back as she looked through the cavity, once again pointing out the stars she recognised. She soon realised there were far more stars visible there than she'd ever seen or even knew existed in the universe.

"Shall we sit by the fire?" Aaron suggested. "Then Spellbound can tell you the story of this place."

Spellbound padded over to the fire, gesturing with his orange paw for them to sit on the fur-covered logs that made quite comfortable seats. As he started to speak the warm glow from the fire and the flickering flames projected a shimmering light from the crystals onto the side of the cave, illuminating the area to expose gold symbols covering large portions of the wall.

Spellbound lifted his paw toward the opening in the roof of the cave. "What you see up there are the many worlds of the universe. The energy of Andalustria has held the balance of these worlds between light and dark and between the power of good and evil since the beginning of time."

The passion coming from the furry orange creature as he relayed his story surprised Eddie and Melody. They looked over at Aaron who nodded in agreement as Spellbound spoke. Assured by the wise man's affirmative response, they turned to face Spellbound as he told his tale.

Chapter 11

The Balance of the Worlds

"The energy from the waters of the Nardor Lagoon and the vibrant luminescence of this pool emanates from the aqua aura crystals," he said, waving his arms towards the silken water at the foot of the waterfall and gesturing around him to the floor of the cave. "These crystals are born from deep within the magical core of Andalustria, and it is here within this Illuminator pool that they are transformed into the iridescent brilliance you see all around you."

As Spellbound spoke they took a closer look, noticing the crystals were not only in the pool but scattered across the floor of the cave and embedded in the walls as well. The variegated shades of white, silver, blue, aquamarine, and turquoise were sparkling and glistening all around them in the dark cavern.

"The magikal energy from the aqua aura crystals is necessary for Andalustria to perform its role as the balance centre of the universe," Spellbound said solemnly. "Without their potent energy we can no longer maintain that balance," he said lowering his head, crestfallen at that possibility.

Aaron moved to sit beside Spellbound. Placing a supportive arm around the furry creature's shoulder he encouraged him to share the worries that plagued his mind, dwarfing the mini-Sasquatch with his embrace.

"Tell them your story, dear one", Aaron said, encouraging Spellbound to open the door to the secrets of Nardor. Heartened by Aaron's support he continued pointing at the apex of the waterfall as he spoke. "You see the aqua aura sphere at the top of the waterfall. That's where the Chalice of Andalustria used to reside." He continued with a deep unhappy sigh, his voice cracking at the words he uttered: "Before it was stolen from this land."

Eddie and Melody looked up in wonder at the massive, empty aqua aura sphere sitting atop the waterfall. Melody wondered how the chalice got inside the large crystal orb in the first place, while Eddie contemplated who might have stolen it and why.

Spellbound continued, unaware of the intrigue and mystery he was generating in Melody's and Eddie's minds. "The crystals can only transform into the luminescent aqua aura gems when the gold essence of the Chalice is infused through the pool's water into the clear quartz. Without the gold essence they remain clear and their energy isn't powerful enough to maintain the universal balance as it does when both elements are synergised."

"Does this make sense to you?" Spellbound asked, watching to see if they understood what he'd said.

"Yes, I understand how merging the two elements so they become one can create a stronger effect," Melody said.

"Me, too," said Eddie, who knew about this from watching Melody's scientific experiments. "It happens with friendship and teamwork, too," Eddie pointed out. "It's much easier and quicker to work out answers to problems when Melody and I work together than if I do it on my own," he said, smiling shyly at his friend.

"That's true for us all" Aaron agreed, "a good friendship, partnership or team can be far more powerful when working together than they can ever be on their own."

"Why are the aqua aura crystals so important?" Eddie asked bringing the focus back to the crystals and Spellbound's story, as he was fascinated by the information he was receiving and wanted to learn more. Eddie understood it was important, but hadn't totally grasped exactly what the crystals did that was so essential to them and the future of the universe. The crystals intrigued Eddie and he felt lighter somehow and more confident, experiencing a profound sense of safety from deep within his stomach when he held them in his hands. He thought that even if that was all they did that was pretty good in itself, but he didn't understand how they held so much power over the universe.

"Aqua Aura crystals vibrate to a certain resonance that impacts the energy of all worlds and their inhabitants," Spellbound said. "Be it insects, reptiles, mammals, human or mystical creatures, the crystals create harmony and balance for us all."

"The crystals' energy encourages inner truth, allowing beings to discover and learn who they truly are. It helps them understand their emotions as well as their thoughts so they can communicate with much greater awareness, using their hearts as well as their logic and intelligence. This allows the highest truth to be expressed between people and creatures throughout all the lands and worlds so they can connect and communicate on a deeper level of understanding by developing healthier environments, which in turn creates harmony and balance across the universe." His furry body grew taller as the attentive audience leaned in, listening with rapt concentration as they took in the significance of his words.

"The vibrations of the aqua aura help the worlds to heal from the damages inflicted upon them; restoring balance and harmony. It protects the auric energies of man and all the creatures of all worlds." Spellbound said, pacing as he spoke and turned to Aaron.

"Do you want to tell them what will happen if we no longer have access to the energy of these crystals?" Spellbound asked, not wanting to deliver the bad news himself.

Aaron nodded, continuing where Spellbound left off. "Without the energy of the aqua aura crystals the worlds will fall out of balance. They will no longer have their protection, nor will they be able to heal from any damage they sustain. Confusion and chaos will increase as species can no longer connect to themselves or each other and they will become constantly distressed and out of balance. Wars will rage as species become ever more fearful; living in reaction to each other and the frenzy of life around them, as the unbalanced and chaotic energy of the worlds impacts them all." Aaron prophesied somberly.

"That's the absolute worst-case scenario, of course" Aaron reassured them, seeing the terrified look on the children's faces. "But unfortunately we've already seen small signs this is starting to happen in several worlds since the Chalice of Andalustria was taken, including within your own world," he said, looking directly at them.

"That's unbelievable! Who would have thought such small crystals could be so powerful!" Eddie said, rotating between his thumb and fingers an aquamarine stone he'd retrieved from the floor. "But what else can they do to help us?" he asked.

"Well, the high vibration of the aqua aura crystals clears negativity from the emotional, physical, intellectual, and spiritual bodies, releasing anxiety and depression by enabling healthy expression," Spellbound said. "This creates a sense of peace and wellbeing for you and your surroundings. It helps beings shine their inner beauty out into the world so they can attract success and above all greater happiness." Spellbound smiled as he delivered happier news after Aaron's words of warning.

"I like the sound of that, tell us more about how they can help us," Eddie said, urging Spellbound to continue.

"The vibration of the crystals clears the way for greater wisdom as they open a pathway to inter-dimensional communication, so that different cultures and species can understand each other and embrace opportunities to collaborate." Spellbound took a deep breath, realising his energy was waning, as he'd been talking for a long time.

"I think we've experienced some of that inter-dimensional communication since we've been here," Melody butted in. "We can understand you and Eddie knew exactly what Ling said even though you both speak different languages to us. Is that what you mean?" she asked.

"Yes, that's it exactly Melody, you understand. The Andalustrian energy allows that level of understanding and communication to happen, due to the vibration of the crystals, and works alongside the desire and willingness of species to truly connect with each other," he said with a big toothy grin as he felt his connection to Melody deepen.

Melody mulled over his statement, then said, "It's amazing that just by synergising the two elements from the crystals and the golden chalice such a powerful force is created and that it has such a huge impact on so many things."

"Yes, these crystals blend the properties of quartz with the properties of gold, it's the blend that produces such an intense energy," Spellbound agreed.

"But it's the *collective vibration of all the aqua aura stones* in Andalustria that generates the power to create the balance for all worlds. It is indeed a mighty force for evolution and elevation, which helps to raise the vibration of all living things," Spellbound said looking deeply into their eyes one by one to make certain they understood how important this was to everyone.

Aaron broke in, "New crystals need to be created through this process to maintain the balance, as each crystal does eventually break down and gets pulled back into the land. But don't worry too much, as it takes many hundreds of years for this to occur."

"But we do need to stabilise the balance as soon as we can, as there are small cracks appearing on the aqua aura sphere – a telltale sign that changes are occurring already," Spellbound explained.

"And we can only stabilise things if we recover the Chalice?" Aaron asked.

All of a sudden Spellbound seemed very agitated: "I need to tell you something awful, I can't hold it in any longer," he said, shrinking into himself and seeming smaller by the moment. Melody wondered what could be any more terrible than chaos and confusion and worlds being thrown out of balance.

"Go ahead, Spellbound, it's time for you to be free of this." Aaron's deep soothing tone encouraged the furry creature to speak out.

"It's my fault … it's my fault that the Chalice of Andalustria is gone," he said looking down in shame and embarrassment.

The long silence that followed made everyone uncomfortable, as no one knew what to say next.

"Why is it your fault?" Eddie finally blurted, breaking the awkward silence.

"Many years ago I journeyed to Andalustria on a quest much like you are doing. I came from your land." he said. Eddie and Melody looked at each other in amazement. How could Spellbound come from their land looking as he did? That seemed unbelievable, they thought.

"It's true, I didn't look like this then," he said, stroking his hands down his furry orange body. "Back then I was a young man a bit older than you, Eddie. Actually, we looked quite similar." He rushed on, eager to share his story now that the silent dam of unspoken words had been released.

"When I came here, Lord Nardor oversaw this land. He held the balance of the worlds between light and dark … and I helped him. I became one of the Knights of Nardor," he shared, his tone and body language reflecting a pride they hadn't seen before.

"I undertook a sacred vow to uphold the crystals' safety and protect the Chalice here at the Lagoon of Nardor. But I failed!" The children listened intently as Spellbound's incredible story unfolded.

"When I arrived in Andalustria I met and fell in love with a beautiful young woman." Intrigued at the thought of Spellbound falling in love, they hung on every word wanting to hear more. "One day she sent word that she had something very important to tell me. But Lord Nardor commanded me to stay here and watch over the precious gems at the Lagoon while he visited another land.

"That was the day everything changed" he said, looking at the floor.

"That day a messenger arrived, stressing the urgency of meeting my love, even if only for a short time so she could share her vital secret. So I made a choice. I went to meet my love." Spellbound let out a sad sigh as he continued.

"But when I arrived at the meeting place she wasn't there."

"I was only gone for a short while, an hour . . . no more." His guilt-ridden voice quavered as he uttered his confession. "But when I returned to the Nardor Lagoon everything had changed." Eddie and Melody edged forward on their makeshift log seats with anticipation as Spellbound took a deep breath.

"When I returned. the aqua aura crystals were scattered everywhere and the Chalice was gone ... it had been stolen. There were signs that Lord Nardor had returned and that a struggle had taken place, but Lord Nardor was nowhere to be seen and since that day has disappeared without a trace." Spellbound looked crestfallen as he revealed what had happened.

"As I told you, at that point I was a Knight of Nardor. But when I tried to leave the cave in search of the chalice, all that changed. For I only got as far as the cave opening and my way was barred by an invisible barrier. Then a voice echoed around the cavern, although I saw no one."

"I remember it so well..." he said sadly. "The voice said '*You made a sacred vow to uphold the safety of the aqua auras and protect the Chalice of Andalustria. But you have failed to uphold your vow. As penance you will be spellbound from now until the chalice is returned to its rightful place here in Andalustria and the balance between worlds is restored.*"

"As the voice uttered those words my physical form changed. Orange fur sprouted all over my body, my hands and feet became paws, my young man's body transformed into the creature you see before you," he said, stroking his soft furry body. "Nothing has ever been the same since that day and I have searched all across this land for the Chalice ever since." Spellbound finished his tragic tale.

Eddie and Melody came over to the sad-looking creature and hugged his warm furry body to support him, as he was clearly upset by the telling of his tale. "That's awful . . . what a sad story, you must have loved her a lot to risk so much," said Melody cuddling him tightly.

"I wonder what happened to Lord Nardor and to the lady you loved?" Eddie asked. He encouraged Spellbound to share more details, feeling as if there were too many loose ends for his liking.

Melody wanted to know more about the woman that had captured Spellbound's heart. But he seemed reluctant to share more about her. Maybe he was embarrassed, or wanted privacy, or maybe it was a secret, Melody thought. *It was very intriguing!*

"I honestly don't know what happened to them," said Spellbound, "she wasn't there that day and no one has seen her or Lord Nardor ever since," he said excluding any further details about his lady or her identity. "It constantly haunts my dreams, as it was my actions that were responsible for what occurred and the situation in Andalustria and across the worlds."

"You certainly had a part to play in what happened, but you have owned what you did and paid a heavy price for it," Aaron said. "Try not to be too hard on yourself."

"Whoever stole the Chalice would have found a way to steal it one way or another. It took a lot of advanced planning as it would have been very challenging to detach the Chalice from the Illuminator Sphere and secretly remove it from Andalustria," Aaron said trying to ease some of Spellbound's guilt.

It's hard to imagine this orange ball of fur as a Knight of Nardor, Eddie thought, trying not to giggle. Spellbound seemed to read Eddie's mind and smiled, breaking the tension from the sad story he'd told them. "I know it's hard to imagine me as a Knight, looking like this," he said starting to laugh, easing the mood for all of them.

Everyone joined in, giggling away as they wrapped their arms around Spellbound in solidarity to support him through the terrible situation he had been living with for all these years. *"It's amazing how having a good laugh about things can really relieve the tension and help put things in perspective"* thought Melody. *What a great insight! That was definitely something worth remembering,* the usually serious girl mused as a wave of exhaustion flooded through her.

"Would you like to join us on our quest?" Eddie asked the furry creature. "It may help you find more clues about the Chalice's whereabouts."

Spellbound looked at Eddie gratefully "That would be wonderful! I'd like that," he said.

"Ok, let's settle down and get some sleep now. We have a long journey ahead of us tomorrow," Aaron said.

So they wrapped themselves in the fur rugs that were scattered across the floor of the cave and settled down next to each other for warmth. And as they lay down and tried to get comfortable, wriggling their bodies around on the earth and crystal-strewn floor they realised just how tired they were after what had turned out to be another adventure-filled and eye-opening day. Eddie tossed and turned far too excited to sleep, whilst Melody quickly fell into a deep slumber.

Chapter 12

Forever Friends We Never Knew We Had

It seemed as if only a short time had passed when Aaron woke them, urging them to gather themselves together so they could carry on their journey. Still rubbing sleep from their eyes, they followed him toward an archway they hadn't noticed before at the side of the cave.

Spellbound joined the procession following closely behind Aaron, carrying a large sack slung across his shoulder. They must look a strange sight Melody thought, the huge long-haired bearded man heading their merry band, closely shadowed by a bright furry orange creature and two young humans trudging along the path that exited the cave.

Nardor Lagoon was nowhere in sight when they exited the cave, as they seemed to have come out in a very different place altogether; the path underfoot was crunchy and even through their shoes felt hard on their feet. The trees and bushes on either side of the noisy path waved branches of green and gold foliage at them and the air felt as cool as an autumn day. The gurgling stream had reappeared and ran alongside them as they trudged along in single file.

Eddie hoped the terrain would change soon as it was tough going underfoot, especially as he hadn't properly woken up yet and felt weary after a restless night wriggling around trying to get comfortable on the aqua aura crystal.

The procession continued in silence for some time, everyone contemplating what lay ahead in this continually changing land. Eddie and Melody were busy concentrating on navigating the path underfoot, trying to avoid the sharpest stones that pinched and bruised their feet when they least expected.

All of a sudden the path stopped abruptly, a steep precipice dropping down right in front of them.

When they looked up they could see the light they'd seen earlier, glowing miles off in the distance. But how would they get there? There was no bridge, no path, no aircraft to fly out of this place; it seemed to be a dead end. Was this the end of their journey?

Aaron turned and smiled at them "Have faith, everything is always provided when you trust and have faith."

Eddie was tired, sore, and grumpy and really wanted to lie down somewhere comfortable and just go back to sleep. He felt flat and despondent as a swirl of emotions rushed through him and he didn't really feel like "having faith," He just wanted it to get easier, he was fed up with the never-ending array of challenges and felt a bit overloaded with all the new and at times scary information he'd absorbed. Right now he just wanted to be at home in his comfy bed, curled up with his dog Missy.

On one level Eddie really did believe everything was provided as had proved to be true on so many occasions. But this was different. This was obviously a dead end, he sighed as a crease formed between his eyes. Frowning, he peered down at the sheer drop in front of him trying to focus on what lay below.

Melody, the more practical of the two, who usually only believed in facts, science, and what she could see with her own eyes, turned toward him with a beautiful reassuring smile, "It will be okay, just wait and see, Eddie."

As he stood on the edge of the steep cliff he realised everything was changing. He wasn't sure how any of it made a difference to him, but things were altering inside him, somehow.

He decided the best thing he could do was not think too far ahead and just stay right here, right now in the present, as really that's all he could do anything about anyway. In a moment of great clarity he realised it is the present that creates the future, anyway!

Looking down at the beautiful valley, so far down he could only just make out the bottom of it, he could still see the light in the distance. Even though he felt flat and grumpy, that light called to him. For he knew deep inside him that it was there he would find the answer to help his mother. He took a deep breath, inhaling the light fragrant air that wafted around him as a gentle breeze blew from the depth of the precipice. He uttered a little prayer to the angels asking for help to get them there easily.

Just as he opened his eyes feeling calmer after saying his prayer in his head, he heard the rumble of wind in his ear as a gust of air swished behind him almost knocking him off the cliff into the valley below.

Aaron caught his arm, steadying him, as a giant white swan flew into view. A statuesque blonde woman who glowed with an iridescent blue light around her, much like the Devas of the forest, sat astride the massive swan.

She looked like a princess, adorned with a stunning crown intertwined with gold that swirled around her head, encapsulating a huge turquoise aqua aura stone that sat in the centre of her forehead.

Just like Aaron, this beautiful, lofty lady held a long staff. Hers looked more like a very long wand made of gold and white metals intertwined to create a large swirling circle at the top. She was incredibly beautiful and very elegant. Just being near her made Eddie pull his shoulders back and stand taller, which somehow made him feel more grownup and masterful.

She has a commanding vibration, enchanting yet soothing, he thought. He felt at peace and totally calm in her presence, even though she was still not within touching distance of him.

Behind her more swans flew in with lady riders astride them. *But she was the queen,* he thought. *Yes, this lady was not a princess, she was definitely a queen. He could tell by the way she carried herself, the way she looked so majestic and the way her energy felt. Somehow he knew she was a leader, just like Aaron.*

She looked straight at Eddie. "Thank you for coming and bringing Melody with you, we have been waiting for you for a very long time, dear Edward," this beautiful woman said as she looked deep into his eyes.

Something was familiar about this lady, what was it, he knew but he didn't know her, or did he?

"My name is Nerela, Queen of the Nemurians. I will help you find your centre so you can align with your purpose as you start to take greater leadership of your life and claim your birth right," she said.

"I will help you feel the peace and calm within as you come into alignment. You are loved greatly by our tribe, as is your mother, my sister. She is also one of us," Nerela explained.

Now he knew who she reminded him of, this lovely creature, this queen astride her giant swan before him. She reminded him of his mother. *How very odd*, he thought.

She said his mother was a Nemurian, how was that possible? What did it mean? How can this be? Eddie quickly mulled over what Nerela said, stunned into silence as everything went round and round in his head. It was very confusing, his mother had never spoken of anything like this before, she had never talked about her family, which now that he thought about it was a bit odd.

Did she know, did she remember? He didn't think she did, although he had a distant memory of a story she'd told him as a young boy that had a familiar feel to the place they were in right now.

"Your mother was a great queen in Andalustria many moons ago, before she chose to go to your land to bring peace and calm to the people there," Nerela explained. "She wanted to help them reconnect and come into alignment, to bring them home within themselves so they were happier and more fulfilled. Then they would be able to take greater leadership of their lives in line with their true spiritual purpose in your world," Nerela explained.

Eddie wondered if Nerela knew that his mother had lost her magik, so she couldn't help anyone find their purpose – or anything else, for that matter. She couldn't even help herself right now.

This thought suddenly brought a flood of tears to Eddie's eyes and he couldn't keep them from streaming down his face. The tears came from years of holding onto the sadness of the loss of his mother, his loss, but hers, too. He took a breath, but allowed the tears to flow as he had been holding the sadness of his mother for a very long time and now these wonderful people, Godlike Sprites, Guides, Queens and Squiggins – whatever they were, they all knew.

They knew all about it, they knew what he had been going through. Even though he always looked on the bright side and wanted to save and help his mother, they knew how brave he was. They knew how much courage it took at times to be positive, to keep going and not give up trying to help his mother. After all, he was only a boy. Even though he was now nearly full grown, he was still just a boy.

And actually he needed his mother too, and he missed her very much. Sometimes it would be nice for him to be looked after and cared for and not have to be the adult when he really wasn't one quite yet. He wondered if other people had this challenge with their parents sometimes, as he often saw his school friends looking as if they had the weight of the world on their shoulders.

He really needed support himself, he needed a teacher that didn't freak out and leave a class full of distraught students when sirens went off that she didn't expect. She should have warned them, she could have talked them through the fear and been there as a good leader would be able to do.

Yes, they really needed what Nerela offered in his world right now. Look what had happened to his mother.

His world had sucked all her magik out of her! She didn't remember why she went there. Or if she did, she didn't have her power anymore, so she couldn't do what she went there to do.

His mother was nothing like this beautiful, bold, strong majestic woman in front of him. Or was she?

Aaron came over and put his arm around him and Eddie experienced his love, the warmth, the care, the safety, flood through him. He felt all these feelings that he'd only ever found in nature, rarely in humans, other than Melody of course.

Never in his life had he felt this total sense of safety given to him by an adult, as they all seemed to be struggling with their own demons, having forgotten nature's and their own unique gifts as they became bogged down by life. Most seemed to flounder around, filling up with things that only made them feel worse, like chasing money, being competitive, and buying things they didn't really need but that filled a gap for a short while.

Or they worked too much, became overly busy, ate too much, or just kept going shopping to keep filling the never-ending hole inside them, where the magik needed to be instead.

You couldn't fill the gap created by a lack of connection with something other than that; nothing else would do it.

How did adults not know that? Children knew all this naturally and did what they needed to do to join all their parts together from a very young age. They were instinctive and just knew what they needed, but then it often got conditioned out of them as they were told they were supposed to grow up!

They were supposed to forget that they are part of nature, too. Forget that rolling around in fresh-cut grass grounds your body and makes you feel alive, full of joy and awakens your senses, reconnecting you to the nature that is as much a part of you as you are of it.

When did adults forget that noticing what's around you so you can be truly aware of the other creatures we share our world with, allows us all to work together? Awareness that helps us collaborate as a team, so we can make our world a better place and be a lot happier in the process.

Why do adults forget, what makes them kill the magik? They don't need to do that, they could so easily bring it into each day very simply, just as Eddie did. He still went to school, still had duties, but he knew that one of his responsibilities was remembering he was magikal. He understood that he could transform his world every day just by using his formulas to connect all his parts first.

Eddie knew his purpose was to remind others, to show them how they could link up simply and easily throughout the day. Then they didn't have to lose their magik and they could feel alive and happy all their days.

Eddie relayed all that he believed to Aaron and Nerela and they nodded their heads in agreement as they looked at this brave young boy who was quickly growing into a young man.

They knew he was special and that he was going to remind the people of his world who they really were, so they could be happier and together save Eddie's world from the self-destruction, sabotage, and abuse they saw happening throughout the land.

They had seen how this had worn Eddie's mother down so that she'd completely forgotten that she was magikal. They knew that Eddie would help them help her, so Aaron and Nerela could play their part to get things back on track as it was meant to be, in nature's order and balance.

"Come, Eddie, we are going to the light, so you can take our messages back with you to your mother to reawaken her. Then she can be the mother she used to be for you, and she can be the queen and leader that is her birth right," Nerela explained.

"Am I coming too?" Melody cried out, fearing she'd be left behind as these wise beings appeared to be completely focused on Eddie right now and she was worried she'd been forgotten.

"Dear Melody, of course you're going with Nerela as well," Aaron said. "You're also here for a reason. Just like Edward, you're also part of the solution. You now have your wonderful straight-lined brain as well as some of our 'waviness' from Andalustria to work with too.

"You and Eddie are a great team, all that you've both been through in your world and in ours has given you the power you need. You can be the difference needed by just being yourselves," Aaron reassured Melody.

Melody blew out a very loud and audible sigh of relief: "Phew!"

Everyone looked at her and started laughing, as this was so unlike the straight-lined Melody Mind of old, – well, from yesterday actually.

Melody saw the humour in her worrying and joined in, laughing louder than anyone else as she realised just how much things were changing in a very good way for her.

She knew how important this was, and how important it was to laugh, have fun and skip and run in wavy lines as well. Her clever brain understood it all, and assimilated and adapted quickly as she ran over and hugged her very best friend in the world, Eddie Motion. What a truly magikal boy he was indeed!

Nerela straightened up and said, "It's time to go."

Aaron gave them a big bear hug as he wrapped them into his brown velvety robes. "I'll see you soon, but now you need to go with Nerela."

As they looked over at Nerela, she raised her staff high in the air and a majestic white-winged creature descended to land alongside Eddie and Melody.

At first they thought it was another swan, but this creature was even more spectacular. The giant white-winged tiger moved in to stand powerfully by Eddie's side. The tiger was so large Eddie's eyes popped. He'd never seen a tiger this big, not even in the zoo, and he'd never seen a white one, never mind one with wings.

But what was he thinking? Things were different here, anything was possible, and it seemed that magik happened as a normal part of life each day. How wonderful it would be to stay here in Andalustria with these loving adults to look after and care for him and Melody he thought.

But he knew in his heart it was not meant to be, as his path was in his homeland, helping people remember. At least he would have Melody by his side.

The white tiger rubbed his head against Eddie's leg, asking to be stroked with his nuzzling, just like Eddie's cat at home.

Then, lifting his head, the white-winged tiger spoke to them in a deep, gravelly voice, beckoning to them to get on his back.

"My name is Erador, climb on board," he said in a voice that purred and rumbled as it wrapped its way around you. Eddie climbed on the tiger's back, moving toward the front near the huge animal's giant head. As he did he tried to find a way to steady himself and grabbed the fur round the tiger's neck.

Strangely he noticed the tiger had an inbuilt fur handle on his shoulders that Eddie could easily hold. His grip was tight as he held on for dear life, trying to stabilise himself before they set off.

Melody climbed on Erador's back behind Eddie, reached her arms around his waist to hold on tight and took a deep breath as they launched into the sky. Soaring high into the air was amazing! How could they ever explain the thrilling feel of the wind on their faces as they jettisoned up into the clouds. They followed closely behind Nerela's huge swan that dwarfed the tiger, making Erador appear as small as Eddie's cat in comparison.

Erador's back moulded to their bottoms and legs. His fur felt soft and warm compared to the sudden gust of cold air that had blasted them in the face at their speedy take off. The tiger's body felt like a soft and comfy pillow under their bottoms, but strong too, and they easily settled in, feeling safe and stable, with no fear of falling off as Eddie looked down to see the valley and meandering stream many miles below.

They were surrounded on all sides by Nerela's ladies, riding their swans in close formation. This made them feel strangely comforted as they flew high above the land below.

Quickly they flew around snow-capped mountains and watched as the stream they had been following merged into a larger river and then into the ocean far below. They soared alongside eagles and other unusual winged creatures that looked over at them, nodding and saluting them in recognition as they flew past. *Or was that just his imagination,* Eddie wondered?

It was funny how he thought he might be imagining things. After all that he had experienced in this land was so far beyond his imagination, he found it interesting that a nod or salute from an eagle seemed unusual.

Over valleys and mountains they flew, through a rainbow whose beam caught the tail of the tiger and followed them as they flew on, ever higher, it seemed. He could see they were heading toward the light and who knew where else? Leaning to the right as the tiger swerved to one side, Eddie was fascinated by the beautiful Nemurian warrior women on their majestic swans. Nerela led the way, beckoning them to come alongside her as they flew through the bracingly cool air.

Eddie couldn't quite believe they were flying at all, never mind on a massive great white-winged talking tiger whose fur felt like silk as it cradled them in their perch upon his back.

"What's really happening? What's this all about? Am I dreaming?" Eddie wondered. Looking over at Nerela, his mother's sister, his aunt, he felt the warm glow of trust and connection growing in his heart, even though he had only just met her.

The sense of belonging he felt in this land with these amazing people and guides was incredible, considering he had really only just met them. *Hadn't he? Or had he met them before?*

So many questions. Now everything is a question that was certain before.

Or was it?

Chapter 13
Triumphing Over Fear

Eddie could feel his excitement growing, but he was also starting to feel a bit anxious and frightened as, yet again, he was venturing into the darkness of the unknown.

He knew most people feared not knowing things, and even if they found something exciting they also felt fear. Deep in thought, his mind kept jumping from one thing to another. He felt Melody cuddling her body into his back, holding him tightly as he perched on this wonderful creature, flying through the air to an unknown destination.

His thoughts and emotions were bubbling to the surface, moving from light into dark. Recognising the warning signals of overwhelm, he decided it was probably a good time to use one of his formulas so he could prepare for whatever lay ahead once they landed.

Whenever he stepped into unknown situations Eddie used his simple formulas to put himself at ease so he felt strong, safe, and ready to enjoy whatever lay ahead. He wasn't sure if they'd work now, as this was the biggest, most hair-raising adventure he'd ever been on. But he was going to give it a go as they'd really helped him in the forest earlier, even though he doubted it would at the time, just following the step-by-step formula made him feel better and turned things around.

He decided to include Melody in his 'Triumph Over Fear' formula, because as he noticed the tightness of her hold around his waist and her heavy breathing, he realised she was probably feeling a bit anxious, too.

"Hey, Melody, shall we create some tangible magik together?" he called over his shoulder.

"Oh, I'd love that Eddie, that's just what I need right now," she answered.

Eddie's formulas helped them become clear about how they were really feeling, which wasn't always obvious when you were overwhelmed or frightened with new or unexpected situations.

As they followed the step-by-step structure they were able to recognise if their thoughts were helping them, or making things worse. Once they identified that they could change them if they were negative and quickly turn things around, it created a bit of breathing space to calm down so they really understood what was going on for them.

Both knew from experience that when they followed the formulas they were able to invent solutions to overcome problems and challenges more easily, as Eddie had done in the woods earlier.

They started by asking each other key questions to bring any worries and concerns to the surface. This helped release their built-up emotion in order to focus their mind so they could find a way through the problem more easily. They enjoyed doing this together, but it was just as easy to do on their own.

They asked each other the questions from Eddie's **'Triumph Over Fear' formula**.

1. **What's the worst thing that could happen?**
"I could fall off this huge flying tiger never to be seen again," said Melody.
"I won't find out how to help Mum get her magik back," Eddie replied.

2. **Is that real or true or likely?**
"Yes, I could fall off the tiger," Melody said.
"Really!" said Eddie "do you really believe that, Melody? After all, you're holding onto me very tightly and it's a very deep crevice we're sitting in on Erador's back."
"Well no, I don't suppose it's that likely is it?" she said, "but it's still worrying."
"Yes, it is, but are you as afraid now that you know it's not that likely?" Eddie asked.
"No, I don't suppose so," Melody said.

"How about you, Eddie, is it true that you won't find out how to help your Mother?"
"Mmmm, well maybe not now that we've found Aaron, Erik and Nerela. Things definitely look more hopeful with their support, but I still don't know what to do right now."
"Maybe you don't need to know what to do right now as you're here, and she's in the other world, so you've got plenty of time," said Melody.

"Yes, that's true," said Eddie, "maybe I could just enjoy being in Andalustria meeting all the enchanted creatures and our new friends."

3. **What would you do if the worst happened, how would you deal with it?**
"What if you didn't discover how to help your Mum, what's the worst that would happen Eddie?" asked Melody.
"Well, I suppose my biggest fear is she might leave us, or get really sick and die," said Eddie as tears squeezed out of the corners of his eyes.
"What would you do if that happened?" asked Melody.
"If she left me I'd still have Dad, and maybe I'd come back here, as there's lots of love and support here. Aaron and Nerela said they would look after us. If she got sick I would ask them to help me. I suppose that sort of covers it, really. I really don't need to worry after all, even if I don't find the answers to help Mum."

Eddie felt relieved as he worked through his fears. He knew this was only the beginning and there were more adventures and lessons to come. Now that he'd talked through how he felt he started looking forward to whatever lay ahead as his mood lifted almost instantly.

But they weren't quite done yet, they needed to complete the 'Triumph Over Fear' formula.

4. What support can you get if the worst happened?

Both friends said each other's name in unison, as they always knew they'd be there for each other, no matter what. Then they named all the amazing new friends they'd discovered in Andalustria, as they both had no doubt all of them would support them in any way they needed from here on in their lives.

"So now we both know it's unlikely our worst fears are going to come true, and if they did for any reason, we know we have wonderful support people and creatures we can call on," said Eddie. "Now we can really enjoy soaring through the clouds to who knows where on this amazing winged tiger."

"Yes, that's true," said Melody opening her eyes for the first time on the flight and finally marvelling at the view. She felt the encouraging warmth of the tiger's body keeping her safe as they glided through the sky.

At this Erador turned his head and looked at them with a toothy grin, "You're learning," he purred.

They both stroked the big tiger, grateful for his warmth in the cold air and for his kindness, as they knew he was one of their friends now, too.

"It's so good to get our fears out in the open, to name them so they're no longer hidden in the dark, like the ogre in the dead of night in the bedroom that's really only your dressing gown hanging on the door when you shine the light on it," Eddie said. "Once you bring the fear out and shine a light on it, you can decide if it's really true, or if it's just your imagination playing tricks and trying to scare the pants off you. And you can work out what you'd do if the worst happened, so you don't need to be so afraid anymore."

"It's wonderful," said Melody, "being afraid can stop us from doing things we really want to. It can stop us from really enjoying our life, too. But we need to do the last bit, remember Eddie?" Melody encouraged.

"Of course, that's the best bit, making your own dreams happen," Eddie replied.

5. What's the best that could happen?

Now that they had worked through their fears and knew they'd be okay, they could focus on creating the best outcome their imaginations could dream up and start focusing on what they really wanted to have happen.

"I would like Mum to reconnect with her true Magik and her family here in Andalustria. I'd like her to remember where she comes from so she could get the support and love she needs, so that she never forgets her magik ever again," Eddie said.

At the same time, he took a deep breath, releasing the pressure of carrying the burden of his mother's recovery that he suddenly realised had weighed him down for far too long.

"And I'd like her to zap her horrid ogre boss, so he knows what it feels like to be bullied and he feels sorry for it," Eddie added in a very child-like voice.

"But what do you want for yourself?" asked Melody. Eddie was very good at helping other people, but often forgot to think about himself, or what he wanted. He often ended up drifting around, unsure of his own direction, as he was too busy focusing on everyone else.

"Oh, I don't know," said Eddie. "I suppose I'd like to develop my gifts and help other people by sharing what I've learned. I believe it could really help them. And I'd love to come back to Andalustria to uncover more from Aaron, Erik and Nerela. I know they have a lot to teach me and I love this land, it feels like home to me," Eddie said with a shy smile on his face as he finally voiced his own wishes.

"Other than that I'm happy, as living life is magikal alongside all the wonderful creatures and nature's vibrant beauty which is everywhere, when we choose to notice. I'm so lucky – I already experience that as I breathe it in every day."

"How about you, Melody, what would you like?" Eddie asked.

"Well, I'd like to explore more of the wavy lines in life to see how I can get them to work alongside my straight lines. That would be very exciting to me, now that I know it's possible," she said, "and I'd like to come back here with you too, Eddie."

Melody realised as she spoke that she was starting to feel quite excited about these new possibilities that were opening up, now that they had worked through their fears.

"What do you mean by working the straight and wavy lines together?" Eddie asked curiously.

"I want to see how my plans and my logic can work together with our imagination and emotions to create wonderful things in life. I am beginning to see that when you put both sides together it's a very powerful combination that creates the magik you talk about Eddie, but in a whole new way," Melody enthused. She was excited, feeling inspired to explore possibilities.

"You are so clever, Melody," Eddie said, admiring how his friend so easily expressed in words what was very much in his heart, but he had no words for.

"Eddie, it's actually you who brought this about using your instincts and intuition to develop tangible magik! It focuses the mind to create a logical plan or a formula alongside creating awareness so you recognise what's happening with your body. Then we can express, release and update our emotions, all the while using our imagination to create what we want!" Melody smiled, acknowledging her very best friend with what she saw as the very truth of the matter.

"Have I really done that?" Eddie asked, his eyebrows rising in surprise.

"Yes, and you've done it all quite instinctively, without even thinking too much about it or why it works. You created the insights and formulas with your own unique magik," Melody enthused excitedly. "Your gifts are very powerful; they help people connect their different aspects so they can work together as a team in a simple, easy, uplifting way," Melody explained.

"Oh," said Eddie, "I didn't realise that's what I was doing with my formulas, they just seemed obvious to me."

"That's because you are nature's child and understand how to generate and use the magik. You know how to really help people feel better," she said, "it's incredibly special what you do, Eddie."

Eddie blushed, feeling warm inside as Melody recognised and honoured who he truly was and the gifts he offered to the world with his natural innocence, joy, and his deep connection to nature.

"We haven't finished the formula," she said, "we were so happy after clearing out our fears, we forgot the last bit. Let's do it now."

Eddie smiled and asked Melody the next question, knowing she wouldn't relax until they'd completed the task at hand, even though neither of them felt fearful any more.

6. **What one thing do I need to think, feel or do to make me feel safe and strong right now?**

Melody jumped in, "I'm going to start writing down all your formulas and insights, as they've really helped us while we've been here in Andalustria. So it's proved to me they really work. Just having an understanding about some of these things and taking the simple steps helped me feel safe and strong.

The wonderful thing about tangible magik is, just by increasing our awareness we become changed. And putting specific formulas into action can change how we think and feel, so we can turn things around very quickly. It's an interesting blend. It really is very comprehensive," Melody stated in what she thought was her very best scientific voice.

"I think it's very important to write them down, so we can share them. Is that okay with you Eddie, as they're your formulas?" she asked with anticipation in her voice.

Eddie beamed. A huge smile spread across his face.

"Of course, that would be wonderful, Melody. You'll be able to put them in order and describe them in a way that's easy for people to understand, far better than I can," he said, feeling grateful for his ingenious friend.

Working together with their unique, very individual gifts, they could share their knowledge and help other people reconnect with the magik so they could improve their lives if they wanted to.

"What about you Eddie, what one thing can you do, think, or feel to help you feel safe and strong?" Melody asked.

"Well, I actually feel fine right now, I don't feel anxious anymore after going through the questions." He realised how true this was as he said it.

"But if I was still scared, or wanted more confidence, then I'd close my eyes, take a deep breath into my body, and remember how safe and loved I feel right now from the understanding and care shown us by our new friends Aaron, Nerela, and Erik," Eddie shared. This would be another thing he could add to his formulas for the future.

"It's not just that I feel safe when recalling and breathing this thought into my whole body; it makes me feel ten feet tall and really excited to start on our new adventures," Eddie told Melody, anchoring the lovely feelings deep within him to call on again in the future, whenever he needed them.

7. How do you feel now?

"I feel great," said Eddie "I've released my fear and can see who and what will support me if I need it, and I am really clear about what I want, which is incredible and exciting," Eddie said.

"Me, too," said Melody, "your formulas really work, Eddie; they turn things around very quickly, which is fantastic."

Once Eddie and Melody cleared their fear, they totally enjoyed the rest of the flight on the majestic tiger. They could feel how much their spirits had lifted after working through the formula. Flying through the air at great speed they felt free as a bird – no, make that as free as a flying tiger!

Rainbows appeared all around them and strange and fascinating creatures flew alongside and below them. They sensed a big black shadow hover overhead and looked up to see the giant raven flying high above, escorting them to wherever they were headed.

Eddie wondered if he'd been with them all along and he just hadn't noticed, with everything else that was going on. It was hard to work out what was real and what wasn't at times in this new land.

Eddie turned his head toward Melody and gestured up towards Chandor the raven, "Did you notice he was there?" he asked.

"Yes. His shadow's been hovering over us since the start of our journey," she said, "even when we were in the forest I caught a glimpse of his dark wings flying in circles overhead and heard a cawing sound every now and then too, so I knew he was there," Melody said.

"Wow, I thought he'd abandoned us when we were wounded," Eddie said, feeling ashamed as he realised he'd judged the raven, who they'd been told by the Zingledibod tree would watch over them. It appeared Chandor had been there all along, just not always within their sight. Maybe it had been the raven that had raised the alarm so Aaron knew they were in trouble.

"I really need to stop judging things," Eddie said to Melody, "things aren't always what we think they are. Sometimes it's actually our own fears that make us jump to the wrong conclusion about someone or something," he said with a growing awareness.

"Whether it's a fear of abandonment, of someone judging us, of not being good enough, or any one of the many fears I've had lately, when we're judging something as wrong or bad it really is often just our own fears isn't it?" Eddie posed the question to Melody as an affirmation of his own findings.

"Yes, that's exactly right," she replied. "If we realise that when we start judging something or someone, that it's actually only our own fears and concerns that are popping up, then we can use your Press Pause formula to release our fears, so we can take charge of ourselves once again," she added. "Then we don't need to judge anyone else, as it's very rarely about them. It's really all about us, and we can always do something about that," Melody said with a big grin.

"It's almost impossible to control anyone else, but we can always take charge of how we respond to things, even if it's not easy at times," she sighed.

Melody felt very proud of Eddie, as well as grateful, as she realised how far they had both come since they started on the quest to help his mother. Was that only yesterday? Who knew, it was hard to tell.

They'd really grown up a lot since the fire drill at school earlier, which showed her very clearly that sometimes it took difficulties and challenges in life to really grow into yourself. She realised that discovering new things about life and yourself helped you uncover what you were really made of, too.

As they reviewed how far they had come on this adventure they realised with a bit of trepidation that they were moving closer to the ground. They started to see more clearly what was going on below as the huge trees thinned to unveil more of the lush land. *Land that was probably filled with more mystical creatures they had yet to meet,* Eddie thought.

Chapter 14
The Source of The Magik

As they started descending Nerela came alongside them. "We'll be landing soon. When we arrive, you will meet Morgana. She is a very wise and powerful medicine woman, or seer. She's a wizardess, although some call her a witch, as she is many things rolled into one. She will be able to help you understand why you are here so you can obtain what you need," Nerela explained.

Maybe I'll find the answers I need from Morgana so I really can help my mother recover! Eddie thought.

As they drew closer to their destination, a flicker of silver light flashed across their eyesight as their sprites flew by in unison. *I must ask Melody her sprite's name,* Eddie thought; *I just keep forgetting, with everything else that's been going on.*

The glen felt enchanted as it opened out to reveal itself amongst the trees that whispered who knew what as they swayed lightly in the breeze. Looking down, they saw Aaron and Spellbound standing in the clearing below. Knowing they were here gave them a really warm feeling inside.

Nerela's ladies held back, hovering in the air, choosing not to land with the rest of them.

Their gentle tiger landed softly. He turned, nuzzling into them and purring loudly as he licked them with his huge warm tongue, making them giggle as they wiped their hands across their soaking wet faces.

They jumped off Erador's back, giving him a big hug as they thanked him. He nodded his huge head and stepped back as Nerela's swan extended its wings out to full span and their queen gracefully dismounted.

They ran gratefully into Aaron's outstretched arms as he enfolded them in his brown earthy robes, stroking their heads and smiling at their exuberant joy to see him.

Spellbound joined the group hug as they reconnected after their separate journeys to arrive at this enchanted glen. Melody was intrigued to know how Aaron and Spellbound got there, as the precipice had appeared to be a dead end. She didn't get the chance to ask, though, as tiny metallic wings whirred round her head as the gleaming silver sprite flew down, landing softly on her shoulder. Mo, as that was Melody's sprite's name, whispered words of welcome in her ear as Eddie experienced the same from his cheeky sprite Erik.

After they reconnected with their friends and felt their feet firmly on the ground they looked around, noticing a beautiful cottage. It sat alongside a waterfall cascading into a stream that meandered in a circle around the dwelling, appearing as if the cottage sat on its very own island.

The cottage had a thatched roof, just like a fairy-book house or woodman's cottage of days gone by. Purple and red flowers trailed around the windows and over the roof, radiating their splendorous cerise blooms in the sunlight.

As they drew near the bridge to cross over to the cottage on the island, a gigantic ogre appeared from nowhere, towering menacingly in front of them. "Hello," said the ogre in a dopey sort of voice, "I am Edward. I watch over Morgana and the energy of the portal."

He seemed harmless enough, Melody thought, *but things weren't always what they appeared here. Mind you, they weren't always what they appeared in their world either* she thought.

"Edward looks after what is precious here, he's filled with goodness and light," Nerela said. "He is one of a pair of twins and his brother in now in your world," she explained. "But his brother is filled with darkness," Nerela explained as they looked up at the mammoth, friendly yet very ugly face.

"It's funny how you have the same name," Melody laughed as she gestured toward Edward the ogre and Eddie. Everyone laughed at their size difference as they stood side by side, Eddie courageously looking up at the gentle giant next to him.

A gigantic belly chortle erupted from Edward the ogre as he looked down at the boy, releasing a very smelly odour a bit like very old fish. It really ponged!

"Eeeew," they cried holding their noses as Aaron and Spellbound laughed even louder at their screwed-up faces.

"Sorry," Edward the ogre said with a big toothy grin, "I must get some more of that fairy floss, I ran out last week," he chortled, not taking himself too seriously.

The thought of the ogre cleaning his teeth with fairy floss sent shrills of laughter through them as they marvelled at this new creature who had already generated so much fun after only a few minutes of meeting them. As they prepared themselves for whatever lay ahead, they both decided they would try really hard not to judge anything by what it looked like in future.

Then their thoughts turned to Edward's twin. *It would be scary to meet an ogre filled with darkness; Edward was frightening enough when you first met him and he was good*, Melody thought.

"Where is Edward's brother in our world?" Eddie asked.

"I am sure you will meet him when you are ready. His name is Rick, but he goes by many other names, too. Your mother knows him, he's been a big part of her troubles lately," Nerela said.

"Rick stole the 'Chalice of Andalustria' and took it with him into your land," she explained. "That was one of the reasons your mother left to go on a mission to recover the Chalice. She left many moons ago and was supposed to bring it back here where it belongs," Nerela explained.

"Ooooh Nooooo," Rang out a loud gasp behind them. "It's no wonder I've haven't found the Chalice in Andalustria in all these years. It's not even here," Spellbound cried out, devastated by the realisation of how much time he could have saved if he'd known that.

"Yes, it was taken from Andalustria a long time ago" Nerela confirmed, "but I don't know the full story around it as it was before my time."

Spellbound quickly relayed his story to Nerela as her Amazonian stature towered over him; she didn't seem aware of the importance of the Chalice to Andalustria.

She was shocked by Spellbound's story as it made recovering the Chalice more urgent than she had realised. "We don't know exactly where the Chalice is on earth, but we know Rick has it, which is why your mother ventured there," Nerela reiterated. "But the dark energy of your world drained her magik, as did Rick. So she hasn't been able to complete her mission."

"So maybe that is why you are all here now?" she said motioning to Eddie, Melody, and Spellbound to cross the bridge.

It would be really exciting to help Spellbound recover The Chalice of Andalustria, as well as helping his mother, Eddie thought.

Rick? Where had he heard that name before? Eddie couldn't quite remember, as his brain was filled with everything that had occurred over the last few days. But he knew he'd heard that name somewhere before.

"You are of both worlds, Eddie, so you can help your mother's mission. But you had to go on your own mission first, so you could grow into yourself and become prepared. Does that make sense?" Aaron asked.

They thought everything made complete sense now, as they nodded in agreement. But it was a lot to take in all at once and brought up even more questions for them.

But there was no more time to think about it, as Nerela beckoned them toward the beautiful cottage. "Come this way, all will be revealed," she said.

They crossed the wooden bridge over the stream, stepping into the circle surrounding the cottage, and waited.

"Take a deep breath," Aaron said, "imagine your heart's desire and ask to receive it."

They did as they were told, feeling a sense of anticipation as they silently imagined all that they wished for coming to fruition.

Eddie wanted to discover how to help his mother. And he also wanted to learn more from the creatures and guides of Andalustria so he could expand his tangible magik.

Melody wanted to understand how the mind, emotions, and body worked together. She loved to learn and also wanted to discover more about "the spirit" too, as people talked about it, but she didn't really understand what it was. Maybe she could help Eddie too, as she really enjoyed all she was discovering in Andalustria.

Spellbound wished to recover the Chalice, restore the balance, and return to his original form, so he could become a Knight of Nardor once again.

Nerela soon brought their attention back to the present moment. "Morgana is a great, wise woman who is thousands of years old. She's filled with the force of nature's magik, she is the wisest person we know. Her charms and potions enchant and support people and animals from all the different worlds. Most of them don't even know she exists, or know that she is doing that for them."

Aaron added, "Morgana is kind and loving, but she can also be very direct and stands for no nonsense. You are very fortunate to meet her. She is rarely here, as she has much to do across the worlds to maintain the finely tuned balance of energy now that the Chalice has gone."

They were all excited and a bit nervous too. What would it be like meeting someone thousands of years old? They both figured she would look very old.

But as the cottage door opened, their jaws dropped as a forebodingly beautiful woman appeared from the arched doorway. Her hair as black as night cascaded down her back in undulating waves. She looked no older than Eddie's mother.

How was it possible she was thousands of years old? Eddie thought maybe anything was possible when magik was involved.

As Morgana approached them, she seemed to glide as if she was floating over the surface of the earth, a bit like a hovercraft, which totally fascinated Melody.

Now the size of a normal raven, Chandor perched on Morgana's left shoulder nuzzling into her collar. His raven plumage mirrored her gleaming tresses as he looked down at them imperiously.

Morgana was swathed in a floor-length medieval robe of green, purple and gold. A wide black belt pulled her dress in, emphasising her tiny waist as the golden buckle glinted in the light. Her high-collared gown fanned out around the back of her neck like radiant peacock feathers in full bloom. At times the collar resembled the lizard's fan that raised up and down at their necks warning predators of their power, just like the reptiles Eddie had seen at the zoo during last year's school trip.

She wore an amulet attached to a long gold chain around her neck. Its design intrigued them. It was a large flat circle of tiny diamonds covered with an intricate gold symbol, resting atop glittering stones that shone rays of light out between the symbol in all directions.

She held a long staff much like Nerela's between her graceful fingers. The staff was gold with an elaborate swirling crest cushioning a sizeable purple gem at the centre of the design. *"I'd like to have a staff like this; it's breath-taking* Eddie thought.

When she spoke her voice reverberated through every fibre of their bodies, causing them to quiver throughout their entire beings. Somehow, though, it made them feel content, safe, and happy. Her mouth remained closed when she spoke; she seemed to be talking to them with her mind, even though they could hear her clearly, as if she were speaking from her mouth.

Melody understood about this sort of thing from movies she had watched. She thought this form of communication was called telepathy, where you could read another person's thoughts and could talk to them by connecting with their mind. She thought it was make-believe, but maybe not!

"Welcome, we have been waiting for you through the ages." Morgana's tone reverberated through them. "Your time has come, you are light-keepers of your world. You will help many others awaken with your tangible magik," she said focusing on each in turn.

As she spoke, translucent beams shone from her body, swirling around to surround them. They knew without a doubt that what she said was true, however unlikely it may seem right now.

Morgana's warm, deep tone felt like velvet stroking their ears as it captured their full attention. She glowed around her edges and flecks of light darted around her as she moved. Morgana's eyes were deep violet like a sparkling amethyst, and her lips were a deep rose-red. She was so exquisitely beautiful that Eddie and Melody just couldn't stop staring at her.

Morgana was a very different sort of beauty than Nerela, who was statuesque, fair, and Amazonian in appearance. Morgana's attraction was deep, dark, frightening, uplifting, and loving all at the same time. It felt as if she were filled with a powerful bewitching magik.

She emitted an intense energy that felt as if she were a reflection of all parts of the world rolled into one person. *What a magnificent creature she was*, Eddie thought.

Melody felt the hairs on her arms stand on end, as the colours around her seemed to sharpen and penetrate her senses, even though she felt as warm and cosy as being wrapped entirely in a blanket on a cold winter's night.

Eddie's vision seemed to penetrate through to another realm as he noticed many transparent spectres around Morgana; her energy allowed him to glimpse fleetingly into different worlds, terrifying and exciting at the same time. He felt a warm glow flush over his body as the blood in his veins pulsed, replenishing his cells as he radiated in this amazing woman's vibrant energy. He could feel every breath tantalize his senses as if he was truly waking up for the very first time.

Spellbound stood rooted to the spot in shock as a strange sensation occurred in his stomach, as if a deep knowing flooded his body. Something about this wonderful, magikal woman was so familiar, yet at the same time quite foreign. He could feel the fur rising at the back of his neck and had to pull himself together as tears pricked the inner corner of his eyes. He realised he was holding his breath as he looked at Morgana.

For some reason Spellbound felt the urge to move forward as he took a very deep gracious, dramatic bow toward Morgana and uttered words he didn't even know were in his head: "Good day, Milady, it is a pleasure to encounter your presence again."

Morgana looked down at Spellbound with a gentle smile "Welcome, it is good to see you; it has been a long time. We are both much changed."

Everyone looked at the two of them in amazement as undercurrents of unspoken secrets passed between Morgana and Spellbound. Spellbound stepped back appearing dazed and a bit shaken, but he said no more. They didn't have time to think more about their unusual behaviour as Morgana continued speaking, commanding their full attention with her presence.

"I am Morgana, I hold the light *and* the dark of all worlds; this world, your world, and many other worlds in between," she said. "I am forever with you, even when you can't see me. You only need ask, help will be provided in ways that best fits you at that time."

While she spoke, bright shafts of purple-green light encompassed her as she transformed before their eyes, beginning with her long wavy black hair turning into straight icy strands that slid down her back like a glacier. Her robes became like coal as they flowed to the ground; her staff transformed from gold to steely silver lengthening to three metres. The metal alchemy rotated as it transformed, twirling itself round the staff like a creeping plant growing up the stem, as an intricate hexagon shaped symbol developed at its apex. The glowing purple stone expanded, shining purple-white translucent beams around them as the stone grew as large as the centre of Eddie's palm.

Morgana's lightly tanned skin changed to a snow white, and she looked terrifying. Awestruck, Eddie and

Melody huddled closer as Morgana's transformation took place.

Chandor's feathers also transformed from jet black to an icy-white colour as he appeared to be intrinsically linked to Morgana.

"Dear ones, do not be afraid, without the dark you would not know the light. The dark holds all your fears, worries and concerns. It holds the energy of judgment, meanness, bullying, and the power and control people try to exert over each other.

"Do not fear the dark, as all people and creatures are made of both light and dark as is the normal way of balance. When we deny our fears and parts of ourselves we see as unfit or negative, we close off, hide and shut away the shadow aspects of ourselves that can serve us in very positive ways once we bring them into the light," Morgana explained.

"Know we are all dark and light as you have seen in me. Once you own your darkness as well as your light, you can then walk in your full power to be the difference you were born to be in your world."

As Eddie stared wide-eyed, watching and listening to all Morgana shared with them, he realised his mouth was hanging wide open. He took a breath to calm himself, shutting his mouth from catching flies, as his mother would say. He realised there was a deep truth in the words this beguiling seer spoke.

"Over many moons my darkness was persecuted with fire and death, until I fully claimed my darkness for its value as well as its challenges. Then I was able to use it for good. Only then did the persecution stop."

They stood enraptured by her commanding presence as she continued.

"When we own and fully claim what we judge as negative, or that which others might not accept in us, then we can bring it into the light to heal. Then, and only then, can we transform our energy to establish a balance that makes us safe, present, and true.

"This is the greatest lesson you are learning to master, young Edward, with your emotions and your formulas, and Melody you are doing so with your mind.

"When people fully connect with their emotions to honour and express them in a healthy way, they can use their minds to focus and become clear about what they really want to create, as well as using their bodies to be fully present in each moment. Then they can take the actions needed to fully express their spirit's purpose. Then the great truth of who they are and who they are meant to be this lifetime becomes apparent as they come into alignment," Morgana explained.

"This is called 'Collaborative Intelligence™' or CQ, as we call it."

"CQ is when you live each day being fully aware as you consciously use all aspects of yourself to work as a team, collaboratively. No part of you is left out, denied, judged, or not expressed. When this happens you step into your full power, so you become stronger, happier, and healthier. You are able to be your true self in a more powerful way than you have ever experienced before," Morgana shared.

"As your parts develop collaboratively, you absorb and understand more, your life becomes enriched by living in 'Collaborative Intelligence™'. Your experience of life becomes ever more magikal." Morgana continued, sharing her wisdom of the ages with them.

Exhilarated, Melody took a deep breath as she listened intently. She understood what Morgana was saying, it made perfect sense. What an incredible journey this was turning into on so many levels.

Chapter 15
Totems of Andalustria

Melody reflected on the wisdom Morgana had shared. She had noticed that when people were clear, focused, emotionally connected, and took passionate action toward the outcome they wanted, then they could make what seemed impossible become a reality.

She knew from her own scientific experiments that people who set goals achieved far more than the ones who didn't. She also knew that if people set goals, but had underlying emotions of unworthiness or didn't believe they deserved to have what they wanted, then it didn't matter how much action they took; things weren't likely to happen the way they wanted.

Melody knew it was necessary to have your mind, your emotions, your actions, and your spirit working together (your purpose) to not only get the outcome you want, but to feel fulfilled and happy about it. She knew this to be true, as she had done experiments with many people in this area.

She also noticed that when people didn't talk or express how they felt, and bottled things up inside them, then eventually their bodies and minds became sick. She knew that every time you had a thought it created an emotion. You might be aware of the emotion, or it might hide away in your unconscious mind. Either way, it was still there.

Melody knew that every emotion people experienced created natural chemicals in the body that either made you feel good, happy, and relaxed or were toxic, making you feel bad one way or another.

Melody also knew that when people bottled up or didn't express, speak, or write out their feelings, particularly emotions that made them feel bad, things didn't work as well. It was just the same as having a tooth ache or not treating any illness for too long; it created problems in life. Your energy decreases, thinking becomes negative, you feel tired a lot and eventually your body becomes ill, as your mind and body are bursting to release pent-up emotions that need to get out.

Sometimes the built up emotions come out all at once in bursts of anger, laughter, or tears. Sometimes they come out in evil or bad deeds, like bullying or hurting other people or animals.

Melody had gathered scientific facts about this over the years and had observed it for herself watching and analysing people. She had stored these facts away, but hadn't really known what to do about them before now.

She knew Eddie's formulas helped people recognise, understand and process their thoughts and emotions. And she knew how important that was, as it already had helped them many times over on this journey. His insights and formulas were so simple anyone could use them to help themselves.

They stood entranced by everything Morgana was saying as she continued: "As people become more in the flow with CQ they naturally draw others toward them who are on the same path, so they can work together, collaboratively with other folk, creatures and beings. As more and more beings uncover who they truly are, greatness evolves and magikal occurrences and synchronicities present themselves, to make the world a more enriching place to live and thrive. True magik from dark to light occurs when living in 'Collaborative Intelligence™' is a normal way of life for people," Morgana said with a radiant smile.

Eddie remembered the dark things he had seen and heard on the news lately, and he recognised the truth in what Morgana was sharing. It was often true; people took far more notice of dark things. Often it was only when bad things happened that people decided things needed to change. So maybe dark things were needed, he thought, or people wouldn't know they needed to change and find the light.

It was like the drills at school that seemed so far away right now, but probably only happened a day ago if time in Andalustria was the same as in his world. It seemed many more emergency drills were needed now to prepare for nature's eruptions causing chaos, or bad people coming into the school. Eddie remembered when they had only had one a year. *There must definitely be a lot more darkness nowadays,* he thought.

So it was important for more light to balance it out, he realised, and he knew he wanted to help do that somehow. Maybe that was his purpose, to help bring in light. Perhaps Melody could do it with him, as it was much nicer to work together. He had no idea how he was going to do that, but he knew he wanted to.

"Eddie Motion and Melody Mind, individually you are great warriors here to show others the way out of their darkness, so they can remember their own magik. Working together, you will create a much greater, more positive impact this lifetime and for many to come." Morgana reflected Eddie's thoughts.

"Just like CQ. When all parts work together... the individual parts are strong, but the synergy of all parts working together creates not just strength, health and happiness, but generates its own distinctive power and a unique transformational energy."

Eddie wondered if Morgana had read his mind and his thoughts yet again, or had he read hers?

Spellbound realised that CQ collaboration Morgana described for people was similar to the synergy that happened between the two elements to create the aqua aura crystals. *It was too much of a coincidence, it must all be linked somehow*, he thought.

"Your mother losing her magik was no accident Eddie. It was meant to be," Morgana said, turning to face him. "It happened so you would make this journey to uncover more of who you are, to learn what you are here to do to help your world."

Morgana smiled gently at Eddie, her big violet eyes flooding warmth into his body as she spoke directly to him, realising it was probably a lot for him to take in.

"Nerela will give you the sovereign feathers for your mother so she remembers who she is, and can overcome her challenges in your world. Then she can overcome the ogre to take her rightful leadership place to help transform the dark to the light, just as you are here to do.

"Your mother is a great queen ... And you are both magikians," Morgana said to the astounded children standing before her.

Aaron, their wise old friend, stepped forward. "You've experienced many trials and gained much knowledge from your encounters in Andalustria, and that new wisdom will return with you," Aaron said "You are already in the flow, Eddie Motion, with your magical insights and formulas. Now you need to share them with everyone," he said as Nerela and Morgana nodded in agreement.

"People may laugh at you," Nerela warned. "They may not take you seriously or may shun you or push you away. They may see you as different from them. They may be afraid of their own dark side overwhelming them. There will be some who are terrified of the light, too, as they may have to give up things they have an attachment to," Nerela advised.

"Always remember that we are here for you both in any moment, even if you cannot see us, we are in your heart. You can come back to Andalustria any time you like," Aaron said.

"We will support you to own and honour the darkness so you can help transform it into the light. You are never alone. Remember you only need to 'Press Pause,' take a breath and connect in the way you show others to do with your formulas," Morgana said as she began to remove the pendant from around her neck.

"Ask us for what you need; we will hear you. Always remember who you are, know we are always here for you," she reassured Eddie and Melody, who were rapidly evolving into powerful young adults.

Eddie and Melody stood in front of Morgana as she conveyed her message, as Nerela and Aaron stood alongside them. Tears of relief, joy, and happiness streamed down their faces as they felt deep in their souls that everything these mystical teachers shared was true.

They hadn't been aware of this 'Collaborative Intelligence™', or even knew they needed it. But on some level they must have known ... as that was why Eddie developed his tangible magik. Maybe that was the whole reason they were here in Andalustria, to *remember, to come home*, to come back home to themselves!

Morgana turned, shining her beautiful violet eyes on Spellbound, who appeared to glow under the light of her smile "Spellbound, you will stay here with us, we have much to discuss," she said creating even more intrigue and mystery. "When it is time you will reconnect with Eddie and Melody for the next quest," she said in a definite manner.

Spellbound gave a deep knowing smile, and waved one arm high in the air, giving Morgana another elaborate bow without uttering a single word.

"It is time for you to return to your world, dear ones," Morgana said, turning to Eddie and Melody. "You understand how to create greater happiness and vitality than you have ever known before, now that you possess CQ. So it's time to communicate your message by living your very best life now," she said

As Morgana spoke her hair returned to jet black, her skin took on its original honey brown as she shone her amazing violet eyes over them and smiled. An intense light of deep understanding washed over them as her wisdom flooded their minds and bodies, allowing them to float up into the air like helium balloons filled with pure joy and delight.

Aaron and Nerela moved closer once they landed back on the ground as Erik the sprite flitted round Eddie's head, popping kisses all over his face. It was an incredible feeling knowing they had these amazingly wise, loving, friends to love, support, and guide them on their mission. It was unlike anything either of them had ever experienced.

Nerela leaned toward Eddie, holding three of her huge swan's sovereign feathers in her outstretched hand.

"These feathers are a gift for your mother, so she knows her sister Nerela is with her, calling her back home. These feather totems will remind her who she is," Nerela instructed.

"Morgana also has something for your mother to re-unite her with her magik. So you need worry no more, Eddie," she said passing the sovereign feathers to Eddie.

Lifting him high up so she could look him in the eyes, his legs dangling in the air, Nerela drew her nephew into her arms enveloping him in a loving hug as she said goodbye to him.

It was only in that moment that he totally understood Nerela really was his aunt. That he was really related to this Nemurian Queen! *How incredible,* he thought, gulping.

Eddie couldn't contain himself any longer. "Wow!" he shouted jumping up and down. Feeling relief, happiness, and complete wonder flush over him, tears of joy rolling down to the tip of his nose, as he laughed and cried at the same time.

Eddie really was very connected to his emotions, just like his name Eddie Motion. He allowed himself to express them in a very healthy way, he kept them 'in motion' so they flowed easily.

He knew he had done what he came here to do, to discover how to help his mother. He'd also gained so many precious life-affirming realisations to take back to his world. As he settled down a fleeting thought crossed his mind. Was his mother suddenly going to grow as tall as Nerela when she remembered who she was? Then he wondered why he wasn't as tall as Nerela; she was his aunt, after all.

On one hand they had discovered many answers and learned things they didn't even know they needed to know in Andalustria. But on the other hand, Eddie had many more questions he wanted answers to, and he was pretty sure Melody and her straight-lined mind was feeling the same.

But for now he was content he had found a way to help his mother, which was the main reason he started on this adventure of discovery. As he acknowledged this, Eddie felt a deep gratitude to the wonderful souls surrounding them.

Morgana placed her pendant over Eddie's head to rest around his neck on his journey home.

"Give this 'Amulet of Wisdom' to your mother," she instructed, "it will reconnect her CQ and fill her once again with her own Andalustrian essence. Its power will replenish her energy, renewing strength as it reconfigures her wisdom, so she can do what she needs to do," Morgana said.

As Morgana placed the 'Amulet of Wisdom' around his neck he could feel its pulsing vibrant energy starting to heat him up, making him tingle all over from his fingers to his toes. His mind became clearer, he felt energized and as strong as Thor the Viking God, while feeling settled and peaceful at the same time. He could see into the future with such clarity and truly understood his purpose now. Everything became clear in his mind and body as he felt the wisdom of re-connection flooding his whole being.

"That's one powerful amulet!" he said as he floated up in the air light as a feather once again. Everyone laughed at the quirky boy who was rapidly evolving into a wise young man.

Melody smiled at her friend, joining in the laughter as she grabbed his hand, pulling him back down to earth before he floated any higher and she couldn't reach him.

Aaron handed Eddie and Melody their own aqua aura spheres that fitted neatly in the palm of their hands. When they held the light globes from Nardor, images they couldn't quite decipher moved about inside each of the spheres. They lit up when held, sending pleasant, uplifting sensations right into Eddie and Melody's hearts. The delightful sensations spread throughout their entire bodies, making their hair stand on end.

"These *Illuminator Globes* will remind you to live with CQ at all times. They are connected to you now to help you expand your own unique magik," Aaron said.

"These totems represent all aspects of you. When you hold them you will feel centred and grounded no matter what the situation. If you forget your Illuminator Globe, you only need imagine the globe in your mind's eye and it will be with you to remind you who you truly are, magikal creatures on a great adventure!" Aaron said as he drew them to him.

Melody held her Illuminator Globe out in her hands, marvelling at the images dancing inside and the exhilarating feelings it awakened inside her whole body. She had never owned anything this beautiful before. It reminded her of the feelings she had when she looked into a star-filled sky on a clear night, revelling in the wonder and glory of the universe. Now she had her very own Illuminator to experience those feelings whenever she wanted. How cool was that! She was curious what else they did, but she had to leave that investigation for another time.

Aaron hugged them goodbye enfolding them in his robes, his long, bristly beard tickling their faces. Feelings of safety and contentment seeped into them, knowing he was always there for them no matter what, as the earthy smell of this kind, loving, man pervaded their senses.

It was time to go.

Erik zipped around Eddie's head and Melody's sprite did the same, whispering loving words of encouragement, reminding them they would be with them any time they chose.

Both children felt grateful, but they were also sad to leave their new friends in Andalustria, even though they knew it was time to go back to their world to begin what they needed to do now. They realised they could help other people be in the flow in their own special way, and they could improve their lives with CQ too, now that they knew about it.

It was wonderful to understand about 'Collaborative Intelligence™' and how it could bring more light into every person and hopefully into their whole world. They weren't sure exactly how they were going to do this, but they didn't need to think about it right now.

Right now it was time to go home. Eddie wondered how they were going to get home, as he couldn't see the Zingledibod tree anywhere, and that was how they'd got there.

He turned to ask Morgana and noticed that another "Amulet of Wisdom" had appeared around her neck, glowing a deep golden colour. Were the amulets breeding?

Eddie didn't need to wonder too long as Morgana touched them both on the shoulder, sending tingles like fairy ferrets running up and down their spine and through their bodies.

"It's time for you to journey back home now. I will see you again when it is time," she said in the velvety voice that resonated throughout their bodies.

With that, she stamped her long silver staff on the ground three times. The ground rumbled and a multitude of coloured lights flew in the air around them as an amazing portal of pulsing energy opened up in the centre of where they were standing. Eddie realised this was the light they'd continually seen flickering in the distance as they made their way here.

"This quest was for you, it was not really for your mother, Eddie," Morgana told him. "Your mother needed to be sick in that way so she could be your messenger, so you could take this journey to search for a way to help her. But really it was all about you, it was your initiation, your journey – not hers," she said.

"You will find your mother much changed when you return. As once you chose to take up the leadership mantle needed to help her transform her darkness to light, she was able to start healing. When you give her the totems from this land, it will complete the cycle so she can come fully home to own her full power once again," Morgana explained. Morgana was glowing brightly now, just like the portal.

"Step through the portal, dear ones, so you can go back home to your world," Aaron directed as he gestured for them to step into the light.

Chapter 16

Bringing the Magik Home

Eddie and Melody took a last look around at the assembly of beings who had quite unexpectedly become very dear advocates and friends.

They waved good-bye, thanking everyone for all they had done for them, holding hands as they moved into the light.

As they stepped into the portal, a myriad of light beams shone around them in all directions. The powerful energy vibrated deep within their bodies. Fresh cool air whizzed by with a loud whooshing sound as they travelled at great speed, just as they had done on their way to Andalustria previously through the Zingledibod tree.

They became light-headed, their eyes watered, and their stomachs felt as if they'd dropped into their feet. Every part of their body vibrated and jiggled with strange sensations, and their eyes popped wide with amazement as they saw different lands and creatures flying past as they journeyed home through the portal.

It was as exciting as the arrival of Christmas, as frightening as Friday the 13th or Halloween, and as exhilarating as a fairground rollercoaster, all at the same time!

Bump! Ouch!

All of a sudden they found themselves sitting bolt upright on the ground in the meadow close to Eddie and Melody's homes.

They rubbed their eyes, then looked at each other and burst out laughing. Their hair was standing straight up on end and Melody's hair had even more curls now. They hugged each other tightly feeling their hearts beating fast against each other after their speedy, mind-altering trip home.

Melody and Eddie looked into each other's eyes and without the need of a single word they acknowledged the life-changing journey they had just taken together.

They realised that while their time in Andalustria had come to an end for now, it had changed them both forever in a way neither of them completely realised or could define right now. They wondered in their own unique ways what it would all mean now they were home in their own land.

They both spontaneously took a big breath, letting things land a little more inside them before getting up, hand-in-hand to start off across the field.

As they reached Eddie's garden gate, his very best furry friend, Missy, his little Maltszu dog, came rushing out to greet them. She bounced up and down like a jumping bean at the circus, excitedly trying to kiss them both on the face with her very smelly doggie tongue.

Out of the corner of his eye Eddie noticed his mother standing by their front door. He gasped in surprise as she ran out to greet them, her eyes shiny and sparkling. Her beautiful hair was full of life once again, flowing in a cascade of gold down the length of her back.

She wrapped her arms around them, raining light, delicate kisses on the top of their heads, as she pulled them in close and embraced them. Eddie marvelled at the smell of roses coming from his mother that stroked and soothed his senses. She smelt fresh and free as a spring day, as if she'd just run through a meadow gathering flower nectar.

Melody winked at Eddie, as tears came easily to his eyes. He knew just by looking at his mother and feeling the vibrant, alive, energy coursing through her body as she enfolded them in her arms, that she had somehow got some of her magik back.

And what was happening with Melody? Not only were more curls starting to appear along her fringe, but she was now winking at him. She'd most definitely never done anything like that before!

Things really had changed since their visit to Andalustria! Eddie wondered what else had changed or shifted. He was so happy that his mother appeared so much better than before they'd left. He'd been so worried for so long and felt totally powerless to help her before.

But incredibly, since they had been gone, it seemed all that had now passed.

He was really going to enjoy telling Mum all about their adventures, as he just knew she would understand now, whereas she would have dismissed such things before.

"We have been wondering where you were," she said.

"I knew you were safe but I was starting to get concerned. It has been a few hours since your teacher called to tell us how upset you were when the emergency drill and sirens went off at school earlier today," his mother said.

Melody and Eddie looked at each other wide eyed with surprise at his mother's words. Really? Only a few hours had passed since they had left this world? They thought they had been in Andalustria for several days at least.

Maybe they had gone back in time in this world. Or maybe the portal allowed them to travel through time? Neither could know for sure, but it was all very interesting.

Eddie's mother looked down, noticing he was clutching something tightly in his hand.

The three sovereign swan feathers Nerela had given to him for her sister, his mother, poked out between his fingers. He held them tightly, knowing how valuable they were to help his mother.

Her face turned snow white as she looked at him, shocked. She took a large gulp of air and suddenly burst into tears.

"Oh, goodness!" she exclaimed as she recovered her composure, wiping the tears from her eyes. "I know where you've been, everything's suddenly coming flashing back," she said.

"This is absolutely incredible!

"My lovely boy, thank you so much for going on your expedition! I can't tell you how much this means to me, you have really helped me," his mother said with a very croaky voice

With a big grin, Eddie handed her the sovereign feathers.

As she took them in her hands her hair turned even brighter gold and lit up as the vibrant light from the feathers flowed gently into her.

She giggled and squirmed with the glee of a young child experiencing the joy of discovery when they try something new, as the energy from the feathers coursed through her, filling her with a whole new level of vitality.

She laughed and chuckled, and then started giggling like a young girl. Her mirth and happiness was infectious. They all started laughing together as feelings of relief and gratitude for all that had occurred coursed joyfully through their bodies.

Once she caught her breath, Eddie's mother exclaimed, "I'm so grateful that you're my son," as she held the beautiful feathers, the gift from her sister that her son had brought back for her. "I'm even more thankful for who you have become Eddie," she said as she stroked his curly red hair with her free hand.

The magik flowed through all of them. Eddie knew that now, as did Melody.

Morgana had taught them that by using Collaborative Intelligence™ to focus their mind, they could manifest more of what they wanted. That when they stabilised and centred their emotions, they became still, calm and truly present in their body, so they could feel more peaceful and energised all at the same time.

CQ really did help them raise their vibration so they could attract more of what they wanted into their life. That had been proven to them over and over again while they were in Andalustria, and they knew it would work here in their land too.

They'd learned that Eddie's insights and formulas and the lessons they'd absorbed in Andalustria could help them develop their CQ so it became easier to know exactly what they needed to do and what steps to take in each moment.

They realised that the more they used Collaborative Intelligence™, the more their own magik grew. Which meant they could make a bigger difference and help more people and creatures in their world. Which they both knew was exactly what they wanted to do now.

As his mother cuddled them to her, Eddie felt the 'Amulet of Wisdom' around his neck start to vibrate against his solar plexus, just above his stomach. Looking down, he saw the light from the diamonds pulsing on and off like a beacon as he picked it up in his hand.

"Morgana told me to give you this pendant, it will completely restore your magik," he said to his mother as he lifted the long chain over his head.

"It's been a very long time since I've seen an 'Amulet of Wisdom'" she said as she lifted it over her head to hang down gently over her chest.

As soon as Eddie's mother placed the amulet around her neck a beautiful blue colour started glowing all around her. She lifted her head up high and grew to stand at least two metres tall in front of their eyes, as she was filled with the deep blue colour emanating from the amulet.

Her clothing transformed and looked similar to the blue-and-white robes Nerela had worn. A stunning gold crown holding a large blue stone at its centre appeared on her head shining blue and white rays all around them from its apex. The Nemurian lights shone out from the crown, making them feel warm and cosy whilst energising them all at once.

She looks like Nerela, but like my mother at the same time, Eddie thought. Melody gasped at her transformation as she shimmered and glowed her many hues of blue, which radiated from her, sending a peaceful yet powerful presence all around them.

"There you are," a voice called out from behind them, as Eddie's father stepped up to join them, "it's been so long my love, it is so good to have you back with us now."

Was his father talking to his mother or to them Eddie wondered. *Surely he should be a bit more surprised to see his mother standing there so tall, shimmering blue with a gold crown on her head?*

Yes, he was definitely looking at his mother, not at him, Eddie thought as he watched his father look directly at the woman he loved. A whisper echoed silently, caressing his ear as a voice very like his mother's spoke to him.

"Your father can't see what you and Melody can see Eddie, as he is not of Andalustria. Your father sees your mother's energy, and as her happiness has returned he's connecting with her in a deeper way now. But he's not able to experience her full magik, as it's not his time for that just yet," the voice within his head relayed to him.

Eddie's father embraced his wife lovingly and turned to Eddie.

"Good to see you two back, your mother was getting concerned," his father said, patting him on the shoulder. Then he did something very strange that he hadn't done since Eddie was very small. He picked Eddie up and swung him round in the air as they both laughed with joy as they'd done when he was a very young boy.

His father put him back down on the ground and winked at Eddie, just as Melody had done earlier, as if they had a special secret that no one else knew about. Then he looked over at Eddie's mother, smiled and said, "Oh, I forgot to tell you, your friend from work called; she said your boss, Rick, has left."

Both the children and Eddie's mother stood very still holding their breath, waiting to hear what his father had to say next about this new, very surprising development.

"Apparently it was all very sudden. He said he was leaving the country and wouldn't be back for a very long time," Eddie's father said, completely unaware of the importance of what he was saying.

Eddie's mother looked at the children with a glint in her eye as they subtlety nodded at each other.

They realised that Rick the ogre, who was disguised as Eddie's mother's boss, would have felt the shift in energy now that his mother had her magik back. Just as Eddie and Melody's energy had also shifted when they discovered who they really were and truly understood what they needed to do.

They realised that no one else would see Rick as he truly was, as Edward the ogre's twin. Even though Rick was really the dark ogre of the pair, the people in this land couldn't see him in his true form without experiencing the energy of Andalustria.

They knew that the people of his homeland would only see Rick as a bully, or maybe an arrogant, unpleasant man who tried to control people and suck their power from them, as he had done with Eddie's mother.

It crossed Eddie's mind that he had probably taken the Chalice of Andalustria with him. They would have to find him, if that was the case, as the chalice needed to go back where it belonged.

They all knew that Rick needed to be found and the chalice returned in order to maintain the balance of energy in Andalustria, which also impacted their world.

This thought was relayed between them all without any words necessary, as they gently nodded in acknowledgement of the truth communicated telepathically between them.

"Your friend said they're promoting you to take Rick's place to be the boss, which is pretty cool," Eddie's father continued, oblivious of the unspoken communication relayed among the others. "So it looks like we've got something to celebrate," his father said.

Eddie's mother took a deep breath of contentment, "We do indeed have a lot to celebrate all around," she said to her son and Melody with a huge smile.

Eddie's father seemed unaware of what had passed between Eddie, Melody, and his wife and continued talking to them in his own wonderful way.

"I told your mother you'd be fine. I told her you were a very resourceful young man and you had plenty of tricks up your sleeve to get you through most scrapes," he said winking at Eddie.

"I think you get that from me and my side of the family," Eddie's father said with a broad, proud grin on his face. "I reassured your mother that you and Melody were probably off on one of your adventures and would come home filled with stories of dragons, demons, and witches," he said, chuckling

Melody and Eddie looked at each other glancing over at Eddie's mother, trying not to smirk, until they couldn't hold it any longer and burst into a fit of the giggles again.

Did Eddie's father know about Andalustria, or not?

Who could tell!

But one thing was certain, right now they were back home safe and Eddie had not only fulfilled his mission to help his mother get her magik back, but he'd gained a whole new understanding of who he was and his true purpose in life, as had Melody.

They also knew they had some amazing friends who would help them when they needed it, which may be sooner than they knew, with Rick on the loose.

Neither Eddie's nor Melody's life would ever be the same as it had been before they visited Andalustria.

Eddie knew his life was filled with deep magik and he was ready to share the wonder of that to help more people and make their world a better, happier place, and Melody knew she was going to help him do that in her own unique way, too.

They weren't too concerned that Rick the dark ogre had disappeared, probably taking the Chalice of Andalustria with him, as they knew they could all work together with Eddie's mother to discover its whereabouts. Wherever it was in this world, together they would find it and take it back to Andalustria where it belonged.

It would mean going on another adventure and facing up to Rick the dark ogre, which was a pretty terrifying thought, but that was definitely for another day!

They knew they'd go back to Eddie's mother's birthplace, that wonderful land where they had so many magikal experiences with their guides. They knew that many great adventures lay ahead of them. And they couldn't wait!

But right now, in this moment, they knew deep down that it would all be okay.

They knew this wasn't the end of the journey. It was only just the beginning!

The Tangible Magik Toolkit

Chapter 1 & 2 - Tangible Magik Insights

- When you feel scared, overwhelmed, angry, lonely, or tired, breathe *into* your feelings to allow them to flow through you instead of holding tightly onto them or pushing them down; this helps loosen their hold on you and allows the feelings to soon pass.

- By running your hands and feet under cool water and imagining washing away any feelings that are causing you problems, you can take charge quickly so you can feel good again.

- **Remember:** No person, situation or event has control of your feelings. Your feelings are your own, no one else's. Situations and people can push you toward certain feelings but only you can decide whether to buy into them. No one else can make you feel a particular way unless you allow or give them permission to do so.

- It is only by taking responsibility for your own feelings that you can do something about them. When you choose to take responsibility for your thoughts and feelings you can help yourself to soothe, change, or update them to work better for you.

- You can't always control what happens to you, but you can learn to take charge of yourself and choose how you respond to a feeling, a person or a situation.

Chapter 3 - Press Pause to Create a New Possibility

Give yourself time and space to reframe your thoughts and feelings.

- Put your hand on your stomach.
- Feel your feet on the floor.
- Take a deep breath down to your stomach.
- Hold the breath in your stomach for 3 seconds (count to 3 slowly).
- Breathe out negative bad energy or anything that makes you feel sad, lonely, upset, afraid, or tired.
- Breathe in sunshine, rainbows, the magik of the stars, or whatever makes you feel good. Imagine stroking your favourite pet, lying cosy and safe in your bed, having fun on holiday or in any special magikal place that makes you feel happy and peaceful.
- Do all this 3 times.

Chapter 4 - Tangible Magik Insights

- When you focus on noticing and appreciating the Magik there is in even the simplest everyday things that are all around you, you feel happier, more energised, and enjoy life more.

- When you feel the ground under your body, hug a tree, or stroke an animal it helps ground you in your body, making you feel safe, calm, and happier.

- When you get close to nature and appreciate all its creatures you can absorb the vital, vibrant energy that nature's environment offers to nourish us all. So you can feel more relaxed, peaceful, and uplifted.

- The natural world and nature's creatures are just like us in many ways, they also experience feelings of fright, pain, sadness, and loss as well as happiness, contentment, safety, and joy, just like we do.

- You don't always need to know why you feel a certain way; sometimes it's more beneficial to just let go of being logical and just experience a feeling in the moment. By freeing your mind in this way the perfect answer can present itself at exactly the right time.

Chapter 5 - Tangible Magik Insights

- In general people need to know what could/might happen, or what is happening, in order to feel safe. Children and adults sense when something is not quite right, so being kept from the truth is often worse than being told the facts in many situations, as it increases fear and prevents us from preparing for what might occur and developing resilience to life's up's and down's.

- Showing interest, acceptance and understanding helps you connect more easily with other people and creatures, no matter how different they seem from you at first.

- When we show others we want to understand them, an invisible door opens to help us develop a connection regardless of our breed or culture.

- Whenever you come across new people, creatures or situations, it's common for your freeze, flight, or fight button to be pressed. So take a moment to take a deep breath and suspend any judgments or fears that pop up. Then you can work out how you would like to respond, instead of instantly reacting to the situation.

- All of nature's creatures are the same underneath, whether people or animals; they all want to be loved, cared for, and accepted just as they are, in their true form.

- When you take time to learn to read the signals of the body properly you can uncover what others are thinking and feeling. Then you can decide the best way to communicate with them, which is not possible if you jump to conclusions.

Chapter 6 - Tangible Magik Insights

- When you let yourself skip around wherever you want and just have fun it makes you feel happy.

- When you think something is a certain way you will likely behave a certain way because of that thought. So check that your thoughts are based on reality and not judgment, prejudice, or out-dated learned behaviour before you act upon your thought.

- You have the power to change the thoughts you have about anything, any time you choose.

- When you get in touch with nature's many textures through your senses; touching, seeing, hearing and smelling the wonders Mother Nature gives us, you reconnect with yourself on a deeper level. This allows you to fill up with vibrant energy and develop a peaceful inner confidence, even in the strangest places and situations.

- Sometimes things that appear beautiful and mesmerizing can be dangerous and bad for you.

- Sometimes things that appear ugly and fearsome on the surface may actually be kind and good for you.

- Never judge what's good for you only by what you see on the outside.

Chapter 7 - Tangible Magik Press Pause Formula (Part 1 & 2)

- Place your hand on your stomach.
- Breathe in deeply through your nose, breathe right down to your stomach.
- Push your stomach out with the air that flows into your body from your breath.
- Hold your breath in your stomach and count to three in your head.
- Blow your breath out through your mouth, making a big whooshing sound.
- Release tension and emotions you may have been holding onto with the out-breath.

Part 2

- Now imagine a time when you felt completely safe and happy.
- Take another deep breath in through your nose and right down to your stomach.
- Let the feelings of safety and comfort flow into your body with your breath.
- Breathe down to your stomach, filling your whole body with these wonderful feelings.
- Breathe out from your mouth, releasing any remaining feelings you no longer want.
- Release any fear, worry, anger and sadness; blow it right out of your body.

Chapter 8 - Tangible Magik Insight

Courage comes in many forms:

- Being brave to take action.
- The courage to be still and calm.
- The courage to be quiet, to listen and observe.
- The courage to be true to yourself and speak up.
- The courage to admit when you are wrong.
- The courage to stand up for what is right.
- The courage to use your wisdom to know when to do any of these things.

Chapter 9 - Tangible Magik Insights

- It is good to experience challenges in life so you can test what you are made of and develop your body, mind, emotions, and spirit to strengthen your skills, gifts, and resilience.

- By learning to deal with and overcome difficulties in life you build your self-confidence and self-belief so you feel a greater sense of achievement.

- If everything is given to you too easily and you don't need to work towards anything to achieve it, you will never experience a real sense of accomplishment, success, or triumph.

- If you choose not to learn from your experiences, or act like a victim and blame others for what happens to you, then you don't allow yourself to grow emotionally and could end up feeling powerless and life may feel sad and very dull.

- What looks like a dead-end may just be a lesson in patience or trust.

Chapter 10 & 11 Tangible Magik Insights

- Even if you are an important person and have important things to do in life, it's vital to allow yourself time and space to have fun and relax to increase your life potential and improve your happiness levels; everyone needs quality down-time.

- A good friendship, partnership or team can be far more powerful by collaborating and working harmoniously together, than if you work alone.

- Choose to take responsibility and own your actions or behaviour; even if you have to admit to something bad, or you're frightened of other people's reactions. Then and only then can you start to positively turn things around.

- Choosing to have a good laugh about things or see the funny side of situations can really relieve tension, and help put things back in perspective.

Chapter 12 - Tangible Magik Insights

- The present moment is the only thing you have control over.

- Release any sadness or regret from the past, let go of worry or concern for the future, as right now is the only place where your power lies – nowhere else.

- When you focus your attention and energy in the present you increase your ability to create a positive future.

- Focus on the present moment, right here right now, so you can take charge of your thoughts, your feelings and your actions. This will increase your body's strength and energy, focus your mind and help you feel calmer and more confident within yourself.

- It is not possible to fill a gap that is caused by ignoring your inner needs of love, safety, warmth, and care by filling it up with money, work, food, internet, or things. This may seem to fill the gap for a short time, but will make you feel worse in the end and doesn't solve the true problem of being disconnected within and to yourself.

- When you connect to your feelings and own, express, and release them *(even if that's hard at first)*, focus your mind on how you want to feel *(your deep desires)* and what gives you joy, then you're able to take action to create more of that for yourself. By doing this, you honour your true nature and can quickly replenish your energy and your magik.

- You cannot fill the gap you feel from a lack of connection with yourself with anything other than that connection and the magik that this brings; nothing else will fill that hole.

- Remember you are a part of nature; allow your inner child and magikal adult out to play. You might do this by rolling in fresh-cut grass, hugging a tree, inhaling blossoms, walking by rivers, the countryside, or the sea. Or you can stroke the hairs on your skin or the fur of an animal, feel your feet on the earth as you breathe in the fresh air, sunshine, or clouds of the day. This reconnects you with yourself so you can feel alive and fill yourself up with joy as you awaken your senses, reconnecting you with your true nature, reminding you who you truly are.

- When you truly connect with yourself, you experience a greater appreciation of others so you can relate on a deeper level than ever before.

- Once you truly notice what's all around you, you heighten your awareness of other people and the creatures who share our world, so you can collaborate as a team, instead of feeling separate. Then your world becomes a better place and you feel happier in the process.

Chapter 13 - Triumph Over Fear Formula

Use this formula to help you to positively manage and overcome fear by asking key questions to bring worries and concerns to the surface and refocus the mind. The questions shine a light on what's hidden or unconscious, while releasing built-up emotions by expressing them. This creates greater clarity to define the support needed to find a way through the problem.

Ask yourself the following questions:

1. What's the worst thing that could happen?

2. Is that real or true or likely?

3. What would you do if the worst happened; how would you deal with it?

4. What support can you get if the worst happened?

5. What's the best that could happen?

6. What one thing do you need to think, feel or do to make you feel safe and strong right now?

7. How do I feel now?

Chapter 14 - Tangible Magik Insights

- Everyone is made up of light and dark, as is the normal way of balance. The dark holds our fears, worries and concerns, our judgment, unkindnesses, bullying, and the power and control people can take and command over each other.

- Without the darkness you would not know the light.

- When we deny our fears or parts of ourselves we see as unfit or bad, we deny our own shadow which, when acknowledged, can serve us well when we bring it into the light to heal.

- As your energy transforms, it creates a balance so you can feel more stable, safe, and present as you step into your full power.

- When people connect with their emotions to honour and express them in a healthy manner, then focus their minds on what they really want to create while being fully present in their body, they're able to take the best actions to fully express their spirit's purpose.

- The great truth of who you are and who you are meant to be in this lifetime becomes apparent as you come into alignment. This is called "Collaborative Intelligence™"

- "Collaborative Intelligence™," or CQ, happens when you live in a state of full awareness, using all aspects of yourself collaboratively as a team within yourself. Then you can step into your full power and become stronger, happier and healthier. The more you embrace "Collaborative Intelligence™" the more magikal life becomes.

Chapter 15 - Tangible Magik Insights

- Every feeling (emotion) you have creates natural chemicals in your body that make you feel good, happy, and relaxed. Or they are toxic and make you feel bad.

- When you bottle up, don't talk about or write out your feelings, things don't work well. Your energy decreases, you become negative, feel tired and your body becomes sick as you're bursting with built-up emotion that needs to get out.

- Emotions that build up can come out all at once in a burst of anger, laughing, or crying. Or even evil or bad deeds like bullying behaviour, or hurting other people or animals.

- It is necessary for your mind + your emotions + your body + your spirit to work together to create the outcome you want.

- Tangible Magik formulas, messages, and tools can help you recognise, understand, and process your thoughts and emotions so you can become happier, healthier, and more fulfilled.

- As you become more in the flow with CQ you draw others to you who are on the same path, so you can work together collaboratively with other folk, creatures and beings.

- CQ = when all parts work together collaboratively. Each individual part is strong, but the synergy of all parts working together creates not just strength, health, and happiness, it generates its own unique magik, too.

Epilogue

When we live in a world based on external achievement, commerce, business, and celebration of the mighty dollar, what place do mystical guides have in everyday life?

How can we work with the long-forgotten, long-yearned-for connection to our spiritual self in a world that is focused on what we own, our position, and what we do in life? Deep down we know this never truly gives us peace.

Remembering the truth of who we truly are outside of any role we play, status we have, or possessions we own; remembering *who you are* when you re-reconnect to your natural essence, awakens your spirit, and opens the way for others to do the same. Aaron, Nerela, Morgana, Erik, and Edward show us, adults and children alike, how to move out of the darkness and into the light. So we can reconnect with our true essence with acceptance, love, fun, magik, and peace... if we allow it to be so.

These qualities invite you to bring *tangible magik* into your everyday life so you no longer need to fill up with over-work, shopping binges, food indulgence or deprivation, or internet cravings, to name a few of the things we use to fill the gap inside of us. Rather, we can decide to make more conscious, empowering choices to enhance our life each day, in each moment . . . .

It is for you to bring the magik home in a tangible way so you can feel its purpose, value, and wisdom in all that you do. It is for you to choose to know your guides and helpers so you can work with them in real time and in your day-to-day life.

You no longer need to feel embarrassed or ashamed of your inner child who so wants to connect you to the fairies, elves, dragons and wizards that are only just behind the veil.

Now is your time to embrace your own "Tangible Magik!"

THE END

Author Bio
Suzanne de Malplaquet

Suzanne is originally from England, the eldest of four children from parents and grandparents in the entertainment world, she grew up exposed to a diverse variety of experiences and personalities. From childhood her finely tuned sensitivity to others combined with being immersed in a world of 'unusual' experiences allowed her natural intuitive abilities to develop and strengthen from an early age.

After creating a successful career in the corporate world she turned to alternative methods of restorative therapies and strategies when she suffered burn-out. She was so impressed with the results that she decided to dedicate the rest of her life to studying and practicing these skills. Combining her business knowledge and skills with her intuitive abilities to 'read' people she opened her own communication wellness business in the UK.

In 1994 Suzanne emigrated to New Zealand and continued her studies becoming a Master Practitioner (AIBMA) *(body language specialist)*, a Counsellor (MIT), Hypnotherapist (HNZDH), Reiki Master and Executive Coach (ICF).

Over the last 23 years' Suzanne has worked with thousands of individuals as well as many of today's leading companies. Helping people to improve their health and elevate their communication to experience greater depth and quality in their life and relationships personally and in the workplace.

Her clients range from Sky TV (UK), Air New Zealand, Qantas, NZ Rugby, ASB Bank to security and surveillance teams at Sky City Casino, China Sands (Macau) and Marina Bay Sands (Singapore).

Suzanne is also the media's *'go to'* analyst: The Body Language Analyst for TVNZ, 7 Sharp, Breakfast TV, TV3's Paul Henry Show, SKY TV (UK) and The Herald national newspaper. Suzanne works alongside mainstream media to report on key figures, was the Body Language analyst for the New Zealand and US elections and is a feature writer in several magazines. She is also co-author of #No.1 Best-selling book *'Align, Expand, Succeed'* and *'101 Ways to Enhance Your Career'*

Increase Your Own Tangible Magik

Now you've experienced Eddie's Tangible Magik
you can download our Press Pause App
to help you keep your own Magik alive!

Free Download (+ paid area optional)
Be Calmer, Connected and Confident

Press Pause to access our *'Tangible Magik Coach'*
to help you

Press Pause to *Take Charge of Life*
Replenish, Relax - *Re-charge Your Battery*
Increase Resilience - *Inner Strength & Power*
Supercharge Confidence - *Increase Self Esteem*
Overcome Overwhelm - *Release fear & Anxiety*
Release Limitations - *Overcome anger & stress*
Increase Results - *Be in the Potential Zone*
Be Change Ready - *Prepare for Change*
Relaxing Sleep - *Rest & Replenish*
Re-energise - *Boost Your Energy*
Enjoy - *Boost the Magik!*

1000's of people around the world experience
huge benefits from the Press Pause App
- Now you can too
www.presspause.today